'In this moving collection, *Writing* corners of marriage, motherhoo home. Domestic spaces are explor versal. These stories are made all attention to her external landscapes. Whether exploring Guyana's jungle-scapes and flat lands, Irish cliffs or rural Wales, her characters arrive on the page eager to tell their stories. They spill off the page in Guyanese patois, in English, in the regional dialects of the United Kingdom; their small intimacies lingering long after the last page has been closed.'

– *Sharon Millar*

Sharon Millar was born and lives in Trinidad. She is the co-winner of the 2013 Commonwealth Short Story Prize and the 2012 Small Axe Short Fiction Award. Her first collection The Whale House and other stories (Peepal Tree Press 2015) *was shortlisted for fiction component of the 2016 OCM Bocas Prize and her work has been anthologised in* Pepperpot: Best New Stories from the Caribbean (Akashic Books). *She is currently at work on her first novel.*

'The title story of a poet discarding a commercially ambitious, feisty alter ego to discover her true creative self in her migrant's fears and memories of displacement, echoes Keats' epitaph for himself as 'one whose name was writ in water'. This paradox defines the book's central theme of loss and gain. An emigrant mother in 'Sending for Chantal' promises for 30 years to meet her daughter 'soon soon', a drowning trafficked African teenager loses his freedom and his life but not his decency, the mother of a troubled daughter realises that her own efforts to help have been a form of collusion. There are women trapped by their false self-image, by class snobbery, or by poverty; yet in the anti-fairy story 'Sleeping Beauty' a mother frozen in anxiety is ultimately released by her daughter's teenage rebellion, while in 'Tellng Barbie' we hear the silent daughter of a 'problem' family telling her beloved doll how they achieve a moment of true harmony and pleasure. In these bitter-sweet, beautifully written tales Maggie Harris, with her poet's lyricism, poignancy and verbal range, invites us, exhilaratingly, to listen to the voices and share the experience of ordinary 'unimportant' people struggling, often heroically, to make the best of difficult lives.

– *Janet Montefiore*

Janet Montefiore, Professor Emerita of the University of Kent, is the author of Feminism and Poetry, Men and Women Writers of the 1930s, *other critical books and a memoir in 50 sonnets,* Shaping Spirits 1948-1966 *(2016). She is proud to have taught the undergraduate option 'Women and Poetry' to Maggie Harris at Kent University in the 1990s, when both of them were 20 years younger.*

For my mother, Elizabeth, my sisters Desiree, Mary, Yonnette – journey women – and my husband, Steven, for catching me when I fall.

WRITING ON WATER

MAGGIE HARRIS

Seren Short Stories

SEREN

Seren is the book imprint of
Poetry Wales Press Ltd
57 Nolton Street, Bridgend, Wales, CF31 3AE
www.serenbooks.com
Facebook: facebook.com/SerenBooks
Twitter: @SerenBooks

ISBNs
Pback – 978-1-78172-370-8
Ebook – 978-1-78172-371-5
Kindle – 978-1-78172-372-2

A CIP record for this title is available from the British Library.

The publisher acknowledges the financial assistance of the Welsh Books
Council.

Printed by Latimer Trend Ltd, Plymouth.

CONTENTS

SENDING FOR CHANTAL

My mother voice growing old over the telephone.

At first I thought was the line crackling, you know sometime reception ain good considering whether the voice have to travel under the sea or over the sky. Then there was also the business of her getting American. That one was a slow business. When pickney small is only so and so they does notice. Like how when Sunday come and we running up to Uncle Marcus house to hear the telephone and Granny complaining at me slow she say, slow, your Granny leg ain fass like yourn. And when we reach and the telephone ring *Bringg Bringg! Bringg Bringg!* and me one cyant control misself is climbing I climbing up high on Uncle Marcus kitchen stool. And when she sweet voice come tinkling down the wire like birdies singing or water down the drainpipe is the sound I holding on to and the words follow.

Chantal! She say, *Chantal! How's my sweetheart honeychile Mummy chocolate fudge eh?*

Sometime she so clear is like she in the room and Granny say the first few time I drop the phone and was looking all round the house for Mummy and bust out one crying. Was like the time we puppy Smartie see he-self in the long mirror and start yapping and running behind the mirror for find the other dog.

Other time her voice ain clear at all, she sound like she shouting through the drainpipe or like the boys on the dam fishing, cupping them hand round them mouth and hollering cross the water. Uncle Marcus shake the phone then and blow down it, and put it to he ear and he face getting vex bad. He have to cut the line he say cos it na good but he don't cut it, he put it down and look at it and then it ring again after a long time when we getting fed up and then all of we jump and then laugh when Mummy voice come back on.

The other thing I remember about the first sound was happiness. Happiness come jumping through the telephone wire like sunshine running on paving stone. Mummy laughing and calling me her chocolate fudge and how she was going to eat me up and blow bubble on my belly like she used to. She even sing me song. She sing me song from movie pictures from flims she know I see, like *we off to see the wizard*. She know I see it because she send me videos. At school my fren them jealous bad when they see I have new videos that ain even in the store yet. She know all the word of them song so good Granny say is like she memorise them. And is true they sound same same, maybe that was one of the times she start to sound American.

The thing that confuse me is this: Mummy happy voice. Because even though I happy hearing her voice dancing on the telephone line, even though Sunday was fill up with all the preparation for that, was still six other days to get through. And a day was a long long time from brekfuss to night. From morning light when other people mummy voice breaking through the jalousie to night-time when them warning *y'all come inside now before jumbie catch you*. I not happy. I want my mummy, the smell of her, the feel of her arm wrap round me even when she push me off she lap and laugh.

That day after my birthday when I was four, when I didn't realise what happening, when the house fill up with uncles and aunties and some cousins from the river and my god-sister who eye turn up funny, when car horn blow and Mummy come out her bedroom with a suitcase and hise me up and wipe ice cream off my face with her kerchief and kiss me and squeeze me she say Chantal Mama gwine away for a lickle bit and Granny gwine look after you and Mama gwine come back soon and collect you ... that day still clear clear in my mind. Before and After not so clear. *Before* mix up with mornings and sunshine and Granny flinging dust out with the broom. *Before* mix up with Mummy have the radio on and going outside with her church shoes on. *Before* was smelling Mummy nice talcum powder smell after she bathe. *After* was Granny use it up till it all gone. *After* was me hollering and not eating and vomiting and kicking Granny.

Was Uncle Marcus say Stop Crying! in he big man hard like rock voice. He say stop my stupidness as I nearing school time and they don't have babies there. He take me out with he in the Govment car and point out the beggars in the street. He drive past the marketplace where the women have their babies under holey parasols in the damblast midday sun while they selling one two mangoes. He drive up the country where the naked skin children playing under the standpipe and he akse me if I want to end up like them. Then he drive me by the seawall and buy me ice cream and tell me my mummy working hard for send me to America.

In school was a white lady teacher. Her voice jump up and down the classroom like balloon when air fizzing out. She teaching everybody to read but some of we like me find it hard. No cat don't sit on no mat in we house. Smartie don't sleep like no log, he sleep like dead dog.

At home postman come with letters from America. Some have my name on them. I spell it out slow, with my finger. Granny read out the words inside and hearing Mummy words through Granny voice was a different experience to the telephone. She write the same things as she say about how she miss her chocolate fudge and how soon she gwine send for me. Sometime Granny slow down she voice and I feel she skipping what else Mummy say. Her lips move quiet then she say how Mummy working real hard, she have to scrub floors and lift heavy old ladies and she hardly don't get any sleep because of Beck and Call. I don't know who they is. She say how Chantal must write. She don't understand writing not for me, I prefer talk to she on a Sunday. When I akse Granny when Mummy gon send for me she say soon soon. When I akse Mummy when she gon send for me she say soon soon.

Come a time we go to Uncle Marcus house and wait but no telephone ring. We sit down a whole afternoon and no telephone ring. That situation last a long time. I know because rainy season come and go and every Sunday we walk down the road rain flooding the road from the trench. Uncle Marcus say he ain driving no Govment car to get stick up in mud.

Day after day the postman ride past the house on he bike, raising he leg and cussing as Smartie take a liking to chasing he. Granny suck she teeth when he don't stop and under her breath she say people tiefing everything these days. Granny start for warn me things is hard, and food get simple, she lining up in the Govment shop for flour and rice. She taking in my uniform the same time she letting it down. Granny get job. She cleaning rich people house up by the lake. Sometime she take me with her, we get the bus and walk down a long road with big gate and button entry. The floor there not like we one. Them so shine I frighten meself looking down. The icebox so big I can fit inside if I have a mind to. Granny point out lobster and clam in freezer bag she say come from Miami.

She assure me my mother is not in Miami.

In my bedroom I line up the things Mummy send me when the postman used to stop, dolly clothes and sweetie, pictures of she standing in snow with a woolly hat on. My finger trace she face with she short hair. The video she send stand up on the windowsill. I only see them one two time, because tiefman come in the house and steal the video-player.

The children them in the yard call me Sendfor. I dint know what that mean for a long time. They not nasty all the time. All o' we play catcher and hopscotch, skipping and dare. Two boy who did use to tease me boast how they really gwine soon and sure enough one day they gone. Granny say they uncle sponsor them to Canada. Somebody else in the yard they call Comeback. Was a girl who aunty take she to London say she would get her nurse job but she come back by Christmas and soon again sitting on the back-steps shelling peas.

By some foolishness there was also a boy call Fallback. They say he mother and father send he from London to learn education and respect back home because children don't listen to their parent there. I feel sorry for he more than me. People tease he because he so poshy poshy talk like English duck and quack quack is all we hear while we laughing until one day he cuff one of the boys so hard he knock he teeth out. After that they play nice and he learn for talk like we.

One day the postman bring not only letter but parcel. Granny hand shaking while she find the scissors and cut careful not to slice the stamps or anything that might be cuttable inside. When it cut, two bottle nail polish roll out. Follow by a pen and pencil set which had sharpener and eraser inside. It nice bad because it had Michael Jackson on it. Granny unfold the letter and go sit down in the rocker. I see words rolling way down the page. When she finish reading she hold it to she chest and start rock. I akse her Granny is what she say is what happen and she only shake she head. I akse she if we can go back Uncle Marcus on Sunday and she say wait and see.

Wait and see went on long. I start high school and Fallback start walking home with me. He tell me how he miss he mother too and I just look at he and look away and don't say nothing. I dint know that what it call, *missing*. In my bedroom I think bout this *missing*. I run my finger over the nail polish bottle and the Michael Jackson pencil set and I wonder if her finger touch them too. I put them to my nose and smell them. I wrap my arms round my old dolly and think about Mummy blowing bubbles on my baby belly.

At school they send me to special classes because they say I dyslexic. The saviour was the computer; I learn that thing so fast they say everybody got to watch out. As time went on computer start for do all kinds thing. Uncle Marcus lucky he still driving the Govment car; he say the best thing in this world is fa keep your head down and work hard. What that mean is that even when Govment change and one batch o' crooks get exchange for another he still got he job. Words he always say was like water and nobody must never waste them neither let them run away. Uncle Marcus buy computer then and so is how we get back in touch with Mummy, only this time instead of telephone go *bringg bringg* is the computer bringing Mummy voice. You have to wear earphone like pilot. The first thing I notice is how she voice changing, not only it not happy but it tired. The second thing was the time it take for somebody to talk and somebody to answer back. I imagine everybody words criss-crossing somewhere in the air. Musee like Luke Skywalker laser. Uncle Marcus say at least it free. Mummy akse me bout school and seem surprise I in high school already. The question I want to akse was trembling on my lip. Everybody waiting to hear it too. But then Mummy said her papers taking a longer time to come through and lossing the job put her right to the back of the queue again. She akse me what I want she send for me and I think, *send for me*. Two week later a pile of magazine arrive. I look at the pictures.

I spect everybody wondering where my father is. Well he don't figure in the Before time. Nobody never call his name. But then come that time when Uncle Marcus get promotion. I remember he drive the Govment car up we road which eventually get fix with tar and stand there proud on the veranda telling Granny he going abroad. Me and Granny jumping up and dancing sure to Jesus is America we gwine see Mummy. But Uncle Marcus hold he palm and pressing it down and say, not we, he. He boss make Consul over in the islands and he say he want he safe honest same driver. He dint know if we can go holiday maybe. I jump up again. Airplane fly out same as Mummy. Bound for drop me somewhere near she!

Some say bout people crawling out the woodwork and that what my father did. Crawl out of some backwood and say nobody taking he chile out the country. Right on the doorstep there was ricketics carrying on and for the first time I like a bone in-between. Between all o' them settle the agreement that this man who name my father go tek he turn look after he own pickney.

And so come Sendfor Chantal realise she have a father. I couldn't see no significance in that. Not everything got significance. And when he come fer me in some bruk-down van I cyan hardly see Smartie tail dropping by the rocker whey Granny sit, me eye so fulla water.

There must have been dealings going on behind the scenes because after he turn up and Granny say I gwine stay the holidays with him I learn she get sick. I was fourteen then and couldn't carry on the way I did when I was four. Though I wanted to scream and shout and kick the way I did when Mummy left I know it would be unseemly. I look at my granny and realise I never even think of her with her own name. Rosa she name Rosa, not Granny. She look small small and her hair getting white.

Them holidays stretched to two year. Granny had to go hospital and then recuperate at her cousin house across the river. They let go we house. The man call my father live way up the East Coast with he wife Mena and three children. They had a farm with skinny cows and mango and jamoon which Mena sell at market. Was she I had to fight shame and tell when I see blood in my panty.

Them three children didn't make themself. That what I keep telling meself when they run tell lie how I tiefing the sugar, how I drop Mena best cup pon the floor. They tell me I lie my mother in America. They say I an got no mother. Mena vex that I cyant roll roti. The school they send me was more backward than me. They never see computer and everybody sharing exercise book.

Nobody round there had no telephone. I trying hard to keep Mummy voice in my head. Over and over I concentrate on how it sound, and how she laugh. Sometime one of the lil girls laugh jus like Mummy. I wake up foreday morning and imagine it was Sunday and me and Granny going up to Uncle Marcus house. I used to akse the man call my father if I cyant visit Granny, he say it too far and the van bruk down.

A line o' coconut tree run the back o' the yard. Behind that the land stretch flat and wild all the way to the ocean. When rain fall plenty it flood. Nobody don't go there. Ghost story fill everybody head when the radio not working or the man call my father cyant get work. He spit on the ground and say everybody abandon the country and if he had a choice he won't live near no slave logies. Mena catch another baby and school was done then for me.

The August I was sixteen Uncle Marcus come back. I hanging out the clothes and see the self same Govment car come driving down the road in a cloud of dust. The car draw up in the yard and the man call my father rouse heself from the hammock saying ah who dat. I know was my Uncle Marcus uncurling heself out the car. He get fat. A smile crease he face and I fly so fast I nearly knock he down. He say how I get big. I stick he in the belly and say how he get fat.

If money change hands that day I don't know. I only know that was one Big Head Queen sit down in that front seat and drive away. I only know that out the corner of my eye I peeping at Uncle Marcus like he's a jumbie. I dint cry at all when I leave the house with my one two things. Funny though all them children start bawling and the lil girl hold on to me tight.

Uncle Marcus house was same same; same kitchen stool which don't look so high. Same telephone sit up there. But pon the table a new computer. Uncle Marcus say we go visit Granny at she cousin but guess who send thing for me! Big box stand on the table. Inside was clothes and handbag, make-up and shoes. *You see she? You see she?* I akse. And Uncle Marcus bring out a envelope and show me photos of when he went America and visit Mummy. And there was Mummy in somewhere call New Jersey. She standing in a room at her godmother house. Her godmother old like Granny and can't walk. You see chile, Uncle Marcus say, she cyant have you there. You still a dependent and she a dependent too.

But Uncle Marcus pick up the telephone and start dial. He saying hello hello, shake the phone and look in the receiver. Then he say hello hello again and he face break in a smile. He pass it to me. I say hello hello too and crackling over the line *a hello chocolate fudge* come over the line. My throat swell up all a sudden and I don't know what I saying. Her voice sounding so different like is stranger I talking to.

Uncle Marcus shake he head when he find out my education was rolling roti and minding chilren. He enrol me in college for learn computer and adding up.

My mummy head fill the Skype screen. At first nobody know what to say. She say I looking big like a proper young woman. I say she hair getting fine fine pon she head. Her voice sound real American now even slow and drawly. Only one two word coming through from hereabouts. Her cheek draw down and her hands fluttering like prayer flags. I want to akse her the question but I know the answer. I want to akse her something else too. I want to tell her bout the programme I watching last night about all them Africans drowning trying reach Europe. We got TV here now and all the time I watching America though sometimes I get fed up with who boyfren do what to who girlfren and who uncle steal the money and car and gun and Hannah Montana singing and dancing and I switch to World News where water swallow up a whole island and terrorist blow up young people in a place call Bali. Instead I talk to she about Fallback. But she don't know Fallback. Only Granny know Fallback. I tell her bout Smartie, how he get drown jumping off the boat that take Granny. She akse me bout the man call my father how we get on and all I can say is all right I suppose. She roll she eyes.

It seem time past when Mummy can send for me. Rules say I now have to apply for visa on my own. But even Uncle Marcus can't find sponsor. He say left right and centre people jumping ship. He drive we by the seawall and say how this country never have no motherland, that why people stamping shooting killing each other. He say he sorry Fallback gone back how he know how I like he. He warn me must be careful now as man only want one thing. He say he sorry Granny depart this world and left me. Water come in he eye then, she his mummy after all. We watch the water for a long time and I thinking how frighten bad people must be to fling themself in boat and plane and cross the sea. Then I think of them who reach and if that land really free and how much them really pay.

My mother voice growing old over the telephone. Her face grow old on Skype. Her hand grow old and shaky shaky on the paper she write me which most times I can't read. But I shout the children say come, you grandmother on the phone, tell she how people building concrete house now, tell she how yall working hard and maybe next year we can send for she.

LIKE LIZARDS RIDE WATER

There was a moment when the men were assaulting the girls that Isxaaq almost intervened. His fists were clenched and he had started to rise to his feet. It was the old man who stopped him. He had put out his hand and stilled him. Isxaaq felt his wrist being pinned to the ground.

Afterwards he was angry with himself, and angry with the man who had prevented him from rising; prevented him from defending the honour of the girls, who all night were staggering out from the back of the truck in tears. Isxaaq wanted to believe that if one of his sisters had been amongst them, that someone would have stood up for her. After all they were not prisoners. They were not here by force. They had paid their way. They had each one of them made sacrifices to be here. Isxaaq thought of his father's pinched face, his mother's tears; uncles and aunts selling cattle, mortgaging their houses, trading labour, time, and honour to raise the cost of Isxaaq's journey. 'Walk good, my son.'

When, in the morning, they had been herded into new trucks, amid dry laughter from men who casually leaned their rifles over their shoulders, Isxaaq had no doubt that anyone who had attempted to stop them would have been shot. As the engines started, bodies bumped against each other, and Isxaaq found himself locking eyes momentarily with the old man. He didn't know what *he* was doing here. Almost everyone else was young.

Isxaaq had walked one hundred miles. He had walked through the desert at night, slept in the shade of rocks. Sometimes he thought he saw others walking too, either before him, or behind him, but he could never trust his eyes. 'Trust no one' was the last thing his father had said. When he got to the meeting point, others bled out of the hazy morning, young men and girls, eyeing each other warily.

They sat and waited outside the village with no name. In the distance goats bleated and villagers stumbled out of half-built houses. The morning had brought camels and trucks stirring up clouds of dust. When the truck pulled up and two men jumped out, Isxaaq was surprised to see that they carried guns. Fear rose in his heart then and he wanted to turn back. Was it really so bad, the life he was leaving? Images of his friends appeared in his mind then: their battered faces and broken knees. The names of the disappeared floated before him. He stood in the shade of the truck as the men walked between them, taking the parcels of money produced from the folds of their clothing. Sacrificial bundles. Bundles born of blood and tears, dust and hope. They shouted hurry up, get in the back! This was not what he had expected, this intimidation. He had expected it would be like riding on a bus. He pushed to the back of his mind the image of the boy who had returned with his mind half-gone, telling tales of deception and robbery, of being abandoned in the desert. He stood wavering between a past and a future that seemed to offer equal despair. The face of his mother appeared before him, the memory of the caress of her hand on his face seven nights ago: 'Be brave, my son, Abu crossed safely. So will you.'

He had climbed up into that first truck with the memory of her words, taking comfort from the fact that his cousin had already successfully achieved this journey, two years ago. Had crossed into Europe; sent money now for his family. Isxaaq held his chin up. He met the eyes of one of the girls, her head wrapped in a scarf decorated with lizards. She glanced away.

They had travelled for days; over unmade roads, which jerked the bones of their bodies, snapped them against each other like sticks. They reached into the small parcels they carried for snacks – biscuits, bread. Shared a diminishing flagon of water. They stopped at night to relieve themselves. First men, then women, by the side of the road. Isxaaq had felt discomfort relieving himself in proximity to women. The women grouped around each other for protection. The laughter of the men in charge unnerved him.

Other times they slowed to a stop; heard voices. Sat stiff with fear. They did not breathe. Isxaaq had no idea where they were but he knew there were checkpoints. He relaxed when he heard laughter. Sometimes he slid the tarpaulin apart. A flash of daylight cut into his eyes. The shapes of men interrupted his blindness. Guns. Forearms. Money. He breathed slowly and let the tarpaulin fall.

The roar of traffic woke him from a distracted sleep. They were on a highway. Isxaaq was ashamed to find his head had drooped onto the shoulder of the old man. The man had looked at him kindly, his eyes saying all that needed to be said. Heat was an unwanted passenger between them; the smell of sweat and body odour composting through underarms and clothing, settling in nostrils, on tongues. Car horns and the roaring of engines accompanied the loud beating of Isxaaq's heart.

They stopped sometime in the middle of the day. The

men banged on the side of the truck, shouting words that Isxaaq did not recognise. The tarpaulin was raised then, and the group looked out onto a crossroads. The countryside was bleached earth; crops had not grown here for a long time. Mountains undulated in the distance. The men shouted again, waving their rifles, and the group scrambled to their feet, their limbs slow to obey. They dropped one by one onto an unmade road.

They waited in the shade of an acacia tree, its canopy filtering the harsh sun. There was no breeze. Nothing but a lizard stirred. Isxaaq didn't know what they were waiting for. The men had produced a plastic container of water and this they passed lip to lip, not caring that the water was as warm as the sweat on their skin. There was no food.

Out of the rippling wave of heat on the highway a vehicle approached. Two vehicles. Four by fours. They came to stop by the acacia tree. Four men jumped out. They too held guns. Isxaaq could not stop the fear that rolled over him again and again. He watched the men closely. They stood together, sharing the bundles of money out between them. Isxaaq thought of his sister's bondage to the merchant in his village. Three years of unpaid labour, so that he, Isxaaq, could be where he was right now. What was to stop these men turning their guns on each and every one of them, and disposing of their bodies in this scant countryside? The image of the mad boy, the one who had returned, came into his mind. He tried to quell his panic through reason. Why would they want to stop this lucrative trade? Word would soon get out. He preferred to think of Abu, the money he sent.

The men were clapping each other on their shoulders now. The first group looked back and gave a wave, a mock salute. They climbed into the truck and headed back the way they had come.

The new men approached them, counting them, and running their eyes over the women. One of them spoke, a mix of English, Italian and dialect.

'I trust you have been well treated,' he said. 'We have a long journey ahead, some four days before we reach the sea. Here, we have food, eat and relax. We leave when it is dark.'

But they didn't leave when it was dark. When it was dark, they told them that the money they paid was not enough for this dangerous journey. They said they themselves would be in trouble if they were caught. They said that others were more ruthless and would hold them whilst they sent messages to their family for more money. But, not them, they did not have time to spare. That's when they had looked at the women. They told them they were fortunate that being women, they were able to get everyone out of this predicament.

The women had begun to scream and shout, rising to their feet and gathering more closely to each other. That was when one of the men raised his gun and shot it into the acacia tree. A branch splintered and hung, its shadow bleeding on the earth.

The man's quiet voice warned them that no one was going to be harmed. This was just a business arrangement.

Isxaaq and the other men were told to sit beneath the tree and relax. The women sat apart from them, their heads in their palms, their cries rising like the remembered cries of birds. But there were no birds here, only the staggered passage of moonlight through the leaves.

Isxaaq took himself back home in his mind, whilst the women were taken one by one into the back of the trucks.

It was dawn before they left. Split between the new vehicles, again under cover. The road rolled away beneath the wheels, beneath their bodies once again in enforced intimacy, the aroma of skin and fear, and now shame. They did not speak.

The smell of the sea came to them at night, long before they arrived. It was cooler, sending a breeze to greet them, rinse them, cleanse them. The cries of seabirds too, entered the world they shared beneath the tarpaulin, like messengers. But when they clambered down, they didn't see the port they had imagined, bristling with ships. Isxaaq did not know what he had imagined. But what he saw was the mouth of a muddy river and some sort of craft that did not resemble anything like a ship. What he also saw was a moving body that reminded him of termites. As he approached he saw that it was people. He and the others turned and raised their voices to those who had brought them here. Their voices rose in unison, their fists too. But the men turned the vehicles around and drove away.

Isxaaq tried to stay as close to the edge of the craft as possible. He refused to be pressed towards the centre. One of the girls who had travelled with him was close by. He recognised the headscarf she wore. He wished she had sat somewhere else. There was barely enough room for anyone to sit side by side.

He could not forget he had not tried to save her.

As they moved out to sea, he began to dream of the life he would live. He knew there would be difficulties. They were heading for the Italian coast. He did not know what would become of them there. He did not want to live in Italy. His cousin Abu had made it to England. That's where he wanted to go. He tried to relax and imagine a future there. He was good with motorbikes. Maybe he could learn to be a mechanic. He imagined his meeting with Abu. He had memorised his mobile number. That was the first thing he would say, when they questioned him. 'I have a cousin, Abu, in London, here is his telephone number.' He knew Abu would back him up; tell the stories of kidnap and torture.

He must have been smiling to himself, as the girl said: 'Are you happy we are almost there?'

He turned to look at her, his shame returning. She had such large eyes. Beautiful and brown. They did not rebuke him. Next to her, a woman was attempting to hold on to her baby who wanted to crawl, who lifted his arms and stretched his body out in rigid protest. All around him were women and children, young men. He wondered what had happened to the old man who had almost certainly saved his life. What was he doing, making this journey anyway? Did he not have children to look after him? Isxaaq looked at the baby and smiled. He would like to have a child like that someday. When he had reached London, become a mechanic, had somewhere nice to live. Someone started to sing a song. It was not one he knew. But it had a lulling quality that led him again to think of his mother and his childhood, just yesterday, close to her knees as she baked *injera* on the open stove.

He never knew if the wind had turned, or if the engine for some reason had stopped. He never knew if water had begun to seep in with the weight of them. But the sea was suddenly leaning dangerously above them. The whole crowd of passengers whom he had only just been looking at, the mothers and babies, young men with their hopeful grins and leather jackets, the crawling, fretful baby, his exasperated mother – their bodies began to plummet into each other with force, knees and elbows and foreheads cracking together with the finality of bone, clothing heavy with water, flesh an upturned cart of market produce in a sudden up-pour of rain.

Isxaaq was lifted away in a large wave of water. He felt himself risen up and then dropped down in turn. Water filled his ears and eyes, his mouth. He tried to beat at the water with his hands.

He did not know how to swim; there were no rivers back home. But his fingers were strong and found something to hang onto. Some fragment of wood and iron wrenched from the craft. But more and more fingers were rising up from the water like fish. Isxaaq fought to keep his grip as others scrambled for a hold, pushing his hand away, coiling with slippery determination around a loin of timber. The waves slapped against all their faces with insistent anger. All around him cries rose like seabirds circling. A child's body floated past, held up by a buoyant plastic diaper.

Lizards were dancing on the water. He was becoming delusional. He was watching his mother pound maize, watching a lizard just an inch away from him on the wall. So still. Basking in the sun, raising one leg and then the other. But these were swimming, they were rising up and down on the water. The girl's head broke the surface; her hand reaching out to join the fists that had already formed there, cupped tight; fighting for space alongside Isxaaq's. He could feel her legs touch his under the water, frantic. Her large eyes filled her face as she recognised him. He felt her hand slip then, lose her grip on the makeshift raft that was holding its own against the battering waves.

With a certainty that had not been present at any time since he had begun his journey, at any time through all the plans of the past two years, through the farewells, his mother's tears, the acknowledgement of debts and futures, through these weeks of driving closer to hope, through the tension of that night at the crossroads: a certainty arose that made him grasp her hand and pin it beneath his.

He could feel himself losing the sensation of his fingers, the oiled slipperiness that was greasing his body, greasing all their bodies. His fingers slipping. Oil from the boat. The girl's scarf came in his vision again, like a flag, almost jolly as it surfed the surges of water, lifting a little with the wind. Isxaaq's right hand loosened its grip on the wood, reaching for the scarf, grabbing it, wrapping it round and round the wrist of the girl, tying her on to the makeshift raft, bracing his body, using his teeth to knot it securely. His heart was lightening, the fear that had accompanied him disappearing. He managed to say to her, 'Hold on', watched the 'o' of her mouth mirror the roundness of her eyes before he slipped away, her gaze holding his, absolving him, lifting the terror away from him, lighting his journey downwards.

THE OTHER SIDE OF THE RIVER

You can believe me or you can believe me not. Mammee always say that truth like water. You got to catch it before it soak away in the dirt. As the Lord is my witness is true true what happen that day, when my mother catch Spanish through the radio.

See me now and I'm a big man in Tampa, Florida. Only that wasn't always the truth. That day I was just playing at being a big man. Truth is, I was a small boy. A small, small boy.

That I was downstairs playing in the yard was only because Mammee was sick. Mammee was never sick. I was always straying somewhere, me and Ignatius. If not in the bush we were on that river. Georgie, she whisper, Georgie, stay round the yard today, me na feel so good, me belly got nara bad bad. And she tell me how to make bush tea and fetch for her. I don't like to see my mother so. Normally is happy she happy as she moving round the place, brushing and sweeping and pounding cassava and always that radio in the background playing loud those Portuguese and Spanish numbers from across the water. Mammee always listening to that radio, she would shake her head and agree and say um hmm that is right, while she sweeping. I grow accustom to that so I don't see nothing extraordinary when she say, watch out for the man in the radio, he coming. Then she lie down and hold her belly.

I don't like to see my mother so. I used to her singing

and dancing up and her little conversations. I used to her up and down our bruk-down steps with baskets of this and that. I used to her swaying down the road heading for the market. I used to her sprinkling water on the dust in the yard and tending her little vegetable patch. Always is only me and her always forever. I am her little man. So she always tell me and this time she say, stay round and mind me, Georgie. So that's how I staying round on the bridge and that's how I see the salesman walking up the track shimmering like wet lizards on the fence after rain. Ignatius stand by me watching me play with the dog I call Dreyfuss. From nowhere that dog had appeared and he become my shadow. You see Georgie, you see Dreyfuss, everybody used to say. Must be six months or so since he come, appearing on the bridge with his tongue hanging out. After I shoo him away twenty times like the stray dogs, still he sit there watching me; is give up I give up and get used to him like you get used to your shadow. He was smart, real smart. He could do anything a dog could do, only better. Not only would he find anything I hide, no matter how I disguise it, even in Mr Patrick field under the cow-down. Not only could he jump almost halfway up a coconut tree if I throw anything high, but he was more than smart, you could see it in his eyes. You could see it how he run from log to log by Mr Alphonso sawmill, nimble as a I-don't-know-what and never fall in the water once.

Ignatius was standing by me that day, watching me show him Dreyfuss next trick, pretending to be dead when I tell him. He lay down and stretch out his legs by Ignatius feet. Ignatius toenails were black. He stood holding that blue rope he find hanging from Mr Patrick coconut tree even though his mother tell him to put it back where he find it.

She bawl him out good, telling him he bringing bad eye and obeah to her door and she would cut his ass to ribbons. But Ignatius hide it under the bridge by we. He like to practise lasso like them American cowboys in the movies. I remember looking up and asking if he not frighten he would get obeah. But he just laugh and curl up the rope one two three time in his hand before he practise spinning, whirling round on one foot and cutting circles between the sky and the dust he was flinging.

Apart from Dreyfuss jumping up and trying to catch the rope, barking loud in his excitement, the place was quiet. Normally Mammee would have the radio on but like she feel so sick she just want peace and quiet.

The salesman walking up the track not wearing no shoes. The reason I know he is a salesman is because he carrying a briefcase and wearing shirt and tie. Plus he was going in and out the gaps, stopping at gateways and taking off his hat. Me and Ignatius stop playing with the lasso and watch him. He got evens. Two people call him inside and two people set their dog on him. By the time he got to us, he was sweating. He could have been sweating anyway, I am not to know. That day was a hot one. He stood on the bridge and fanned himself with his hat. Was an old felt hat with a red ribbon. His shirt was white and his tie and trousers black. His feet were the same colour as the road.

Morning young mens is your mother at home?

Is who aksing? Ignatius tongue sharp.

I didn't volunteer any information. I just stand there with my hand on Dreyfuss head. Then I realise that Dreyfuss gone quiet, he wasn't baring his teeth like he usually do to strangers.

Thinking back now, I am positive the salesman specifically asked for my mother. He didn't ask for my father. He didn't say, Morning young mens, is your father and mother at home. Perhaps I put too much significance in that. Later, when I wondered where he himself had come from, I would just accept that he knew there were not many men about.

I have a guitar that sings to me now, from the top of the wardrobe. Nobody believes me of course. It is 2014, and I am a big man selling real estate in Tampa. Nobody believes these things anymore. That guitar sing to me just like that radio sing to my mother.

There were not many men about for a reason. And that reason, my friends, was that river. Forgive me if I can't tell you all those other stories that keep me awake at night. Forgive me if I also am unable to name the exact place I grew up. Ha, excuse me, old habits die hard, and names are one of them. No point in digging up all the spite that the dust keep down. Of all the stories, this is only one, although I must add that at the time it wasn't a story at all, it was just one day in my life.

That life was lived on the banks of a river the Portuguese and Spanish had settled for many generations, tearing it between them like a dog with a bone, interrupted sometimes by the French and Dutch, and finally the English. Until Independence of course (if you can call it that) but this story isn't dependent on any of that. Or maybe it is. What they all had in common was that river, and of course you can see why, look on any map and rivers do a good job of marking a territory.

It always seemed like another world, that river, even though I knew our shoreline as intimately as I knew the fingers on my hand. Even though I spent my days upon it. It wasn't only its incandescence in moonlight, the romance poets like to write about from the safety of their attics. It was the very fact that it spirited young men away who were never to return. It would spirit me away too, only I didn't see it like that then, on the contrary it would represent the highway to opportunity.

That river had qualities of its own, independent of what or who it brought, or what or who it took away. Bright mornings would see it shimmer like silver; they said fair-maids shed their scales during the night, that's what gave it its sheen, and just before sunset you could see their shapes forming on the ripples the water threw up like our giant otters, their backs lit up by the dying sun. Listen to me now and you would think I was a poet! Ah oh our slippery tongues! Ha! Only women and old men would say these things.

The men who crossed the river went in search of dreams. Not many returned. Of the exceptions who did, they returned minus limbs or teeth or their minds, the courtesy of piranha or explosives or gunshots. Stories returned with them, of cigarettes extinguished on the backs of women who had skin like armadillos and didn't feel a thing. Violence returned with them and they eased it away in Marvellous rum-shop. Very few returned with diamonds. Of the few that returned with diamonds, Marvellous was one. His rum-shop was frequented day and night by the living and the dead and salesmen bringing Bibles and aluminium saucepans and fragrant soaps and radios, some small enough to hold in the palm of one hand. Of the few that returned with diamonds, Mr Alphonso was another. He had unearthed enough diamonds to build himself a brick house with a veranda where he sat and watched the water writhe from sunrise to sunset. But they were the exceptions.

We lived in a house like any other, my mother and me. A wooden house on stilts. The land flooded at least once a year, and brought alligators out looking for an easy meal. There were two rooms upstairs and a cook-room downstairs, a mere square of bricks where Mammee lit fires for the pot.

In my earliest memories my mother is Mama Wata combing her hair by the window. It falls, thick and black over her shining shoulder, hair and skin both glistening with coconut oil after her evening shower. She is forever singing. That is how I acquired my love for music, listening to my mother sing as I lay half-awake in my cot. She accompanies the radio to Carmen Miranda and Clara Nunes and Alfredo Sadel, rousing choruses accompanied by violins and guitars pouring through the windows even as the night falls and the crickets begin.

I can't let the salesman bother my mother when she sick. I stand before him on the bottom step and shake my head. No, I say. No my mother not home. But the salesman hold his hat with his two hands in front his belly and circle it round and round, his thumbs sliding on the ribbon. His briefcase sit on the ground like a dog between us, waiting. Then my mother voice drop down through the side window. Georgie? Georgie, somebody there? Before I know it the briefcase float up into the salesman hand and he start to climb the steps and I have no choice but to stand aside and watch him place one bare foot after the other climbing up. I went to follow him, my foot getting ready behind his, but his hand stay me, say, stay boy, and I was my mother's little boy, not her little man.

That was when Dreyfuss start to whine, one mewling after another, he sound like a baby. Shush Dreyfuss I say. Ignatius try to tempt him with the lasso. He whirl it round and dangle it like a promise high above his head. Another time Dreyfuss would have leap on that rope like a chicken hawk on a fish head. Leap with his jaws snapping open like a alligator. But now he just keep his head down between his paws.

Ignatius and me both jump when we hear my mother cry. Both of us rush up the steps and I remember chiding myself what stupidness catch me to let a complete stranger enter our property and enter the sanctum of my mother!

The salesman was sitting at the table with his briefcase open. It disappoints me to see there is very little in it apart from a few jars of coffee and a scattered stack of records. His eyes catch mine and he laughs, a note of money fluttering between his fingers. I turn to my mother who is no longer lying in her bed as I left her, but fully standing, looking the same as she did the day before and the day before that. I remember thinking, what use are records? We have no record player; but the salesman's voice distracted me.

Speech! He said brightly, there is a time for speech! And my mother took on the coy look of a girl and twirled the edge of her hair with her fingers.

Ice, young man, ice! The salesman instructs me. Your mother and I have just conducted a successful exchange. My eyes move from my mother to him, and to his fingers where the money still flutters. As I watch, my mother walks closer to the table and lifts a record out of his case. There is something about the way she walks. She's not quite touching the floor. My eyes are drawn to her waist where a narrow red ribbon is firmly tied in a reef knot.

When I come back with the ice the salesman was gone. I would only find out that Dreyfuss was gone later, because the problem I find with my mother then was that she start to address me in Spanish. Of course I did not speak Spanish myself but I have heard a few words from the radio through those love songs that constantly wail words like 'te quiero', and 'amar'. From that day onwards Mammee speak nothing but Spanish. That was to cause a lot of confusion in my life. So much confusion that it would lead me to Tampa, Florida, with my father's guitar. But that is another story.

I search for that dog. I search for that dog in every trench, every doorway, every upturned boat. I beat down the bush with a cutlass at the back of our house and shout his name. I holler his name with my cupped hands from the banks of the river until next morning Mr Alphonso beckon me up on his veranda. Because fear had already filled my heart with the appearance of the salesman, the occurrence of my mother speaking completely in Spanish, and the disappearance of Dreyfuss, I wasn't frighten to climb up Mr Alphonso doorstep and sit on his veranda. I forget all those things people say, how he half-mad searching for diamonds and gold and get infected by mercury. I forget all those other stories what come back with the half-men. I only look at Mr Alphonso, a old man in a Panama hat sitting on a cane chair, and watch him suck tobacco smoke from a clay pipe. Boy, he say, Boy, and he clear his throat and move his eyes from the pipe to the river where the dolphins were question marks riding behind the fisherman's boat. Boy, you mother, she deh? She get better nuh? And I say, yes Mr Alphonso, she deh. I want fuh tell him 'bout the Spanish but the words they jes stick up in my throat. And he say, don't concern yourself with the dog, boy. Your dog done he business. And he turn and watch me with he yellowy old man eyes and he say, you don't get something for nothing in this world boy. Remember that.

These days, driving round Tampa, a city far removed from those shacks and nights full of the songs of tree frogs where sunset drop sudden and the scales of fairmaids light up the river like slices of silver moons, is a far cry, this city of noise, these main roads blasting their pistons like gunshots, the never-ending explosion of hip hop and country and Memphis preachers, these sidewalks and front yards and driveways where I pull up to climb steps made of stone to knock on front doors which will be sometimes opened by housewives with their hair in curlers or balancing babies on their hips, or by disgruntled men rustling newspapers and adjusting their glasses, where the open door might offer a glimpse of a blue pool shimmering out back. So many sum me up in one look – another fast-talking salesman in a sharp suit with a leather briefcase and shining, polished shoes. But there is another me, oh yes, *you know*.

BREAST

Sometimes, the child at her breast makes Marie feel she is being eaten alive. The gums in the small mouth clamp on like a limpet's teeth. Marie would flinch, her fingers torn between smoothing the baby's cheek in this new terrible love, or peeling him away, brushing him away like a creature that had strayed onto her body, an ant perhaps, or a spider.

This flesh of hers, these swollen glands with their raised veins and blue nipples, the rush of milk that would gush like a spring after tingling; hormonal, chemical messages that set the act of feeding in motion, had become a creature itself. It had nothing in common with that long ago, slight rise in her school shirt, the tiny expectant nipples.

'Fried eggs,' he had said, laughing. That first time in the cinema. There was nowhere else dark, or private. The back seats were filled with rustlings, boys' arms 'accidentally' dropping over the shoulders of girls, their thin straps. There he was, that brown-skinned boy, that handsome boy with the white teeth. That was when her body had become a bitch, a treacherous, deceitful bitch.

In the shower her hands strayed over her fourteen-year-old body, rubbing soap slowly over her nipples, watched them harden. Relived the feeling of his mouth on them, his closed eyes, the way he seemed to feed on her with his whole self.

All she knew then was desire and love, her gauche limbs

more used to riding bikes and skipping rope, become a traitor, leading her to mirrors and dress shops, caressing fabric between her fingers, slipping into cubicles to try on selves transformed by satin and chiffon.

The trying on of bras became a sensuous, thrilling ritual; lace and cotton vied for her soul in curtain-drawn mirrored cubicles, conflicted with other thoughts which fought for her mind – becoming an artist, enlightenment, sensible shirts.

Her mother, slipping in the shadows, pushed exercise books and pens in front of her. 'Don't court trouble,' she warned. 'Trouble will find you quick enough.'

A summer pregnancy; discovery coming quick and fast: an extra dimension to sensuality, her small bird eggs, size 28, flushing into a size 34, a generous cup, a hand held cup, her husband's mouth watering at the size of them. Climbing the steps two at a time like Rhett Butler, daytime sex, sunlight pouring through the curtains. Her life becoming cooking and shopping, homemaking. Her drawings packed away in the loft like Christmas decorations, whilst she planned menus, polished the wedding photograph, her white dress billowing like sea spray on a wild day. His surprise, at her orgasm, her breasts spraying his face like a sudden summer shower.

Beauty thy name is Woman.

She learned to walk with understated undulation. No more the sinuous movie star in miniskirts or pedal pushers, neat ankles in Russell and Bromley stilettos. That self, with the flowering breasts, the roller-curled hair, the bleached highlights, the eyes dark and smoky, spidery Biba eyelashes, had morphed. Her body shape sculpted to commas and colons, flags, a ship's figurehead, wind-buffed sails on mercantile seas. The aureole on her breasts widening, darkening. She became a vessel, a cargo ship, a market woman with baskets of produce. She belonged to traditional cultures on far-away continents, Asian, African. When she stooped, she did so with her hand on her back, with slow grace, ready to lean into rice waters, or pluck soft-winged tips of Ceylon tea. Her passage was a flotilla, a precious cargo, a carving space, a load-bearer. Crowds parted.

Today is the first Day of the Rest of your Life.

From nowhere, mantras begin to appear. They manifest themselves in the waiting rooms of doctors' surgeries, x-ray departments, movie screens. There was no one moment she could place. Perhaps moments had begun to morph too, like her body.

Summer, 1976, Covent Garden. The baby had arrived in the spring, came silently into the world, whilst Marie slept, her small-boned body unable to birth him naturally, a transgression that had altered the timeless image of a woman screaming her child into being. Whilst she slept and dreamt of names, the surgeons inked, slit, sliced, lifted, stitched, glued and mended. Their faerie personas interrupted her morphine-fed dreams, so that Rhett Butler became Rumpelstiltskin, midwives became Godmothers who leaned over her willow-woven, skeletal crib with tea-stained teeth.

The first Cut is the Deepest.

She had never felt so beautiful. The baby transformed her into a different being. Beauty sung through the pores of her skin. Her breasts were golden, filled with milk and honey. Surgeons and nurses stood by the side of her bed and told her how amazing she was, You lost so much blood, they said. And look at you, breastfeeding. Caesar mums don't usually take to it that easily. And the baby slept. The baby did not cry like those others, those ugly bald-headed gnomes belonging to other women who trudged up and down to the nursery at night and begged the nurses to take over, let him have a bottle I don't care, give me a sedative, I just want to sleep. No, Marie's baby is a proverb. He nestled into the cushion that protected the thirteen stitches that mended the wound he had initiated, thirteen fairytale woven stitches, fused with catgut and blood; and lay his small dark head obediently against her flushing skin. He was content to be a proverb, slept like a baby should; only opening his eyes at the immersion into water, a temporary scowl marking his otherwise perfect face. She wanted to call him Angel, like the Archangel, but her husband told her not to be silly, everyone would think he was a pooftah, make his life hell. Johnny Cash didn't know what the hell he was singing about. They compromised and called him Michael. And on a summer's day in Covent Garden she sits on the edge of the square, opens her blouse and feeds him. Feeds him easily and unashamed, an innate knowingness flowing through her body as natural as blood and water, in the diametric shadows of coloured balls raining the air. No one is staring. Neither the jugglers nor musicians nor the Mexicans in red velvets and corduroy, with panpipes. They are all as high as she is. Everyone is smiling: the scruffy guys with their long hair and leather sandals, the girls with their rainbow-coloured knitted hip bags, the women in broderie anglaise and denim skirts, elderly couples in light linen, seeking the shade. Their smiles graduate to her and her archangel nestling at her breast.

She is getting used to the attention. She had not been prepared for it. Everywhere she goes. Michael asleep, snug on her back, or, in his pram, arms flung, curled florets of fists against white frilled cotton. They peer at him like messengers, bear him gifts of love. Ask his name, how old he is, are in awe of his beauty. She learns to tell time in weeks and months. Unwittingly she has become a goddess. She sits him up and his eyes blink into the sunshine.

It was the Best of times and the Worst of times.

Her breasts have become their own being. Sometimes she feels they are udders, and she is a cow waiting to be milked. They know when Michael is hungry, the milk rushes in, an odd mixture of sexual desire and release.

Her young, eager husband, mesmerised by her milk-filled breasts, her new voluptuousness, who had held his child with trembling thumbs of love, who came breaking through the door at the end of each working day, was stood outside the circle.

Her breasts are no longer his. He has lost the copyright of his touch. The patent had been lost to a leeching of soft pink gums. And Marie no longer likes him touching them. When he touches them, milk leaks, and this time it isn't a turn-on. Even if he perseveres and rises above her like a bull, she wants him to hurry up and finish, listens out for the small whimper from the baby's room.

Best for Baby, Best for You

Africa is in the news. Africa is always in the news. She forgets what tragedy, what famine. Only the images remain; babies' round bellies, their mothers' haunted eyes, the loose skin of their breasts. The brown-skinned boy comes to mind. If I had married you, she thinks, I would have had a brown-skinned baby. She goes to the library and looks for multicultural literature. But there is no multicultural literature.

Nestlé is on the news. Nestlé in Africa, Asia, China, South America. Smiling mothers on screen-high posters hold up the tin and all the mantras. Best for Baby. Best for You. Mummies no longer need to stay at home. Breasts have been made redundant. All that free love had to be paid for somehow. Women are more than bedfellows. They want to be in the boardroom too. Buy suits and walk like men into the office, their breasts bound. Marie holds her second baby, listens. What we want is a happy baby and a happy Mummy. In the nursery they put the baby on the bottle without asking.

Somehow the climate is changing. From where does the natural occurrence of young mothers and bountiful babies feeding in parks, restaurants, or hotel lounges become incidents shrouded with indecisiveness, a growing self-consciousness and fleeting, secretive glances of shame?

Here now is baby number three. Choices have become life and death decisions. Marie eyes the paraphernalia of bottles, cups her breasts in each hand. Reads literature on contamination. To vaccinate or not to vaccinate. Brain damage. Measles. Whooping cough. Cot death. How to lay your baby down, Michael on his tummy. Effie on her side. Sophie on her back.

From those first static images – drawings of the baby in-vitro, week by week, month by month, thumbed excitedly through the pages of *Mum and Baby* magazine, time has speeded up: technology: the first scans, real life photos of a foetus in the womb sucking its thumb. Pro-Lifers. Abortion clinics. The twelve days she had spent in hospital with Michael, drop to nine for Effie, five for Sophie.

After a Time comes another Time.

Her breasts have withdrawn into themselves. Her husband, tired of her tiredness, nappies and bottles, leaves her. Page Three girls look down at her from the newsstands laughing.

By the time Marie has the cancer scare, she has moved from size 8 to 16; her breasts are a voluptuous weight of mangoes, watermelon cushions of glory. Husband number two rests his penis between them reverently. She looks down at his balding head and the way he suckles, like a baby with his eyes closed.

Her daughter Sophie texts her the images of her scan at 11 weeks. Freely shares it on Facebook. Dresses in tight leggings and tight t-shirts, belly exposed, no Laura Ashley anywhere. There is no way I'm breastfeeding, she tells her mother. Disgusting!

The machine traps her breast between its plates. She had never known such pain. Tell a lie. Twice she had mastitis. Twice. Her breast hard as a coconut. The baby unable to feed. Her face red and angry, her tiny fists flailing. Bathing them in warm water, trying to express the milk.

The tabloids groan with breasts. The models preen like male birds between the pages, sure in their identity, using the sale of their bodies as promotion, aiming to become singers and actresses, MPs and scientists. A hotel asks a breastfeeding mother to leave.

The doctor's face is expressionless. He must have to do this a million times, she thinks. A good life, carry on. You can do without breasts. Breasts don't make you a woman.

Marie stares at him silently. He is a kindly man. Ultimately, it is your choice. The latest evidence ... there's a strong possibility that HRT causes cancer.

Thinking of husband number 3. His pleasure. Imagines a life alone.

I'll take my chances, she says.

She walks out into the street, the exhibition poster catching her eye: *Whose Breasts are These?* She enters. Comes face to face with portraits, magazine images, sculptures, Mother Goddess effigies, broken busts and rotund bellies, archaeological treasures. A bra draped on a clothes hanger. Time rolls away on the rubber floor. And then the one you could touch, a cast of a real woman, a living woman, a thalidomide victim with no arms, and one breast. She traces the figure silently, running her fingers over the rounded contours, the belly of harvest, the breast of gold.

As she leaves, another woman is staring at the poster. She is dressed in black from head to foot, only her eyes are visible. There is light in her eyes. As Marie turns away, her eyes fall to the woman's feet. Beneath the burka, a pair of silver shoes, sparkling.

At home, she reaches for the loft ladder, pulls it down. Somewhere, amongst all the mementoes, baby photographs, medals and cups for ballet, her drawings are waiting. She imagines them stirring, waiting for the moment she opens the box, lets in the light.

SLEEPING BEAUTY
A Caribbean Tale

Sticks and stones. Sticks and stones may break my bones but words will never hurt me. So Carlotta was saying to herself. She hugged her new baby close, walked with her up and down the hallway, stepped out on the veranda to give her some breeze. She looked down at this new perfect creation: in the newborn girlchild's eyes the universe swum, lakes and rivers, clouds and forests. Her eyelashes curled against her dark skin like ethereal palm leaves, lit by the moon. Her dark curls swirled like a shoal of seahorses. Carlotta looked out over the yard where the bougainvillea scrambled over the bruk-teeth fence, vivid purple splashes. The red flowers of the flamboyant spilled over the side gate. A balloon from the party was caught up in the mango tree and bunting was hanging crookedly between them all. Marti would have to put an axe to that bougainvillea, it was climbing up the coconut branches wild and fast. She cast her eye over the yard – it could all do with a tidy up, plastic glasses were strewn over the lawn which itself needed cutting, the water tank was leaning, and parts of Marti's motorbike littered the concrete. He would have to move all that now. Before, he would suck his teeth at her when she raised the subject, *Carly, is a work in progress. You calling it washing-machine parts? Well when you and me speeding down the highway you would feel like a queen then right!* Some Englishman disappointed with the island and plagued with debts had given it to him.

When you have a new baby your time wasn't you own. Carlotta had already realised that. Before, she had had all the time in the world, the office job was just filing and a little computer work. All the years she and Marti were trying for this special baby she'd been advised she mustn't do too much. It wasn't that her body was delicate, but she mustn't have too much stress, body and mind had to work together. Despite the slightly disreputable backyard, they never thought the place was all that bad. She and Marti always used to call it 'their little kingdom'. Was they and they own, and the minicab business brought them enough to live a good and decent life, especially when he had an airport or cruise-ship run. But when a baby born work get plenty, and the party last night had been a celebration without too much planning, from the time when people coming round wanting to wet the baby head, to them deciding, well all right let we have a little party.

Who would have known how it all would end up? They'd been planning a proper party, a proper christening, which was gon be at St Mark's Church when Andreatta was six weeks old. Carlotta had picked out the christening gown even before the baby was born but didn't want to tempt fate, had had Cave Shepherd Department Store put it by with a little down payment. Well who wanted to surprise her and walk in last evening with the gown! Her very own Aunt Mel, her sister godmother! Carlotta didn't even know how she know bout the lil get-together. It seemed everybody hear Carlotta and Marti were holding party for the baby. Carlotta lost count of how many times she repeat, was only a little ting, the *real* celebration was the christening, September month end, at St Mark Church and was going to be proper invitations too. But one after the other they climbed the front steps, neighbours and relatives from as far apart as St Philips and Bathsheba. Carlotta had had to send out to get more food from the Trini shop, nuff people like roti Bajan style, especially when rum was flowing. Even with all the lack of preparation, everybody was having a real nice time, the baby passed around from arm to arm to be kissed, blessed, palm crossed with silver, and in some cases US dollars. The musicians from out the back all come round with drums and shak shaks and guitar. Marti had had to stop them plugging in the sound system because he kept saying wasn't a proper party yet.

But then, in the midst of enjoyment, trouble come. Trouble catch a hire car and come. Trouble walk down the pitch road, cross the gap, take short cut through Millicent back alley, push through nextdoor washing line and come. She walk with she high heel shoe right up Carlotta and Marti front steps and through the gallery where Carlotta swinging Andreatta in the rocking crib.

'Well,' she said. 'Well.' And hand on hip, look down on the group who one second ago were chatting, eating roti, and handing out blessings to the child.

'Well,' said Trouble, 'is a time when some people get so big-up they can't remember them old friend.'

Carlotta looked up, puzzled. 'And you is...?'

Trouble laughed, a backyard laugh which men hate and women fear. She sucked her teeth long and slow.

'So you na remember me even? You na remember you godmother self?'

Carlotta thought quickly and searched her memory slowly. Godmother? The only Godmother she had known, Aunty Brenda, God rest her soul, had passed long ago. Apart from a silver crucifix and a white bible which her mother,

God Rest her Soul, had put by in the sewing machine drawer when Carlotta was growing up, and apart from one or two Aunties and friends of her mother who said Good Morning in church or passing in town, Carlotta felt shame to acknowledge she couldn't remember this one. Part of her didn't like what she was seeing, an apparition the wrong side of fifty, voice slurred, in a red party dress, matching shoes and silver handbag. She didn't seem anyone her mother would have chosen, but then again, her mother was now on the other side and not here to testify. Carlotta also knew that even for Godmothers times and years take their toll and the person who may have been found suitable thirty years ago was not necessarily suitable now. However Carlotta had been well-brought up, her father had used to say it does not matter where you come from, is who you is, an edict that had always kept Carlotta holding her head high. So breeding made her rise, and breeding made her say, I'm sorry I can't remember you but welcome to our house. And breeding was just about to offer Trouble a drink when Trouble's eyes went travelling round the room, noting the happy revellers, the pictures on the walls, the new sofa and sound system, and the small pile of presents on the coffee table.

'Well,' she said. 'Well. Not only was me not invited to the feast, not only did me not say to meself, all right they might did forget me, lemme go anyways. Not only did me catch hire car and walk down the long road past all them nasty chattel houses and past these big-up concrete house with electric gadget galore, all at my own trouble and expense, but now me find,' she paused, and closed her eyes, gathering herself from a rapid breathing which was seeming to overtake her; 'now me find me own godchild na even know me, na even remember me!'

She opened her eyes and raised her arms on which the silver handbag swung. She waved her fingers as if adjusting invisible gloves. 'Well let me leave y'all something y'all won't forget.' She leaned over the rocking crib where the baby's deep-sea eyes had suddenly opened, meeting the malevolent brown stare above her. 'You, my child, you my bright-eyed child, make the most of this pleasant life for it won't last. You will live as if dead then you will be cut up, cut up I tell you! Only one thing gon raise you, my child, and it won't be no prince!'

A cackling rose into the air, a cackling whose volume rose in the room, and travelled through the open windows, out into the yard where the boys were singing, and entered Marti's ear just as he was about to join in. The sun chose that moment to disappear behind a cloud, taking its warmth with it, and everyone, both in the yard and the house, shivered. For a few moments confusion reigned, nobody knew what had gone on, how the place suddenly grow cold, who the old woman in the red dress with the handbag was who marched past them and out the gate. Marti, when he rushed inside at the sound of Carlotta's piercing scream, found his wife holding their baby close to her breast and crying uncontrollably.

The people them had been in uproar, the men ready to chase Trouble out on the main road and bludgeon her to death. But she was long gone, disappearing like the black clouds that had swooped down, bringing winds from nowhere and emptying the yard of revellers. The few who stayed were vociferous in their responses.

Eh eh! But is how woman like that can just waltz in and curse a innocent baby like that!

Demons live amongst us! The Lord Jesus has departed!

We gon catch her ass and skin her! My uncle is a policeman, he can find out who she is.

Best get Father Patrick round quick bless this poor child.

Now this morning, Carlotta comes out onto the veranda, singing and talking to her baby girl, watching out for any danger waiting to snatch her from this world.

She had already worked the house, had got up at dawn and cleared every floorboard, every shelf, every drawer, putting anything that could harm her baby out of reach. She knew it would be a while before Andreatta even crawled, but she would be prepared. The yard would be her next agenda, and Marti, however much he complained, would tidy up that mass of scrap metal he called a bike.

And so began Carlotta's anxieties. Even though the police informed them that Trouble was a madwoman from St Vincent who had last been seen on a cargo boat heading out to sea. Even though all the good people in her life would constantly reassure her that Good overcomes Evil, that words have no power to cause harm, and blessings were sought from pastors, priests, a saddhu from Trinidad and even a obeah man from Guyana. Holy water was sprinkled; incantations dispelled the evil back to whence it had come. Worry entered Carlotta's skin and bone. Endless contemplation caused her to hear voices and engage in conversation with unknown and unseen persons, (a development which Marti tried his utmost to prevent from becoming common knowledge).

The baby now, Andreatta. She had grown into a charming child, a personable, well-mannered child who although cosseted, protected, and loved to the point of distraction, had let none of that infringe on her character. Due to the fear of her mother, she had been educated at home. Carlotta's fear would not allow her to send her daughter out into the world, anything might happen. The curse had said she would be cut, and Carlotta had taken this literally, placing sharp things out of her reach, scissors, knives, opened corned-beef cans, needles, nail files. They used no glass, no china crockery. The thought of broken glass or cracked cup slashing that perfect sapodilla skin filled Carlotta with horror. They used enamel and plastic and Carlotta did not care what anyone thought. When Marti presented her with a bright red Le Creuset saucepan, she wept.

Over the years, the bungalow had been improved, another bedroom added, another bathroom. A water feature in the shape of a mermaid had been cemented into the garden, and the palisade fencing had been replaced by a brick wall, with decorative inserts and scalloped edging. The flamboyant and the bougainvillea, the mango and the coconut had all grown tall and wide-leaved. In fact it can be said that Carlotta encouraged their wild proliferation. They grew from both inside and outside the wall. They cast shadows on the new patio, took the bite out of the sun. More importantly, it prevented anyone looking in.

Marti now owned a fleet of minibuses which took tourists to and from the cruise ships and on tours to North Point and Harrison's Cave. Carlotta was bought gold bracelets and earrings and an Apple Mac on which she took online courses in shamanistic cultures.

Andreatta, until the age of sixteen, had been quite happy with her secluded life. She had more dolls than she could play with, and dolls houses, and Lego. Children and friends of children came visiting by the score, cousins and friends of cousins, came marching through the alleyways and backyards, came via the highway, and poured through the door. But more and more Andreatta's face turned to the gate that led to the outside world, she spied the young men and women going down to the beach, she heard their laughter.

She wandered the enclosed garden kicking stones, her shoulders hunched.

Marti turned from the window at the sight of his daughter peering through the gateway.

'We can't keep her away from the world any more, Carly,' he said. His voice was sad and tired, his hair turning grey. He had thrown himself into his work which had taken away some of the worry, but the toll it had taken on his wife was much worse. 'I think we need to forget this madness now, and let her take her chances.'

'No!' Carlotta shouted. She flew at Marti, and forced his hands into hers. 'We can't, Marti, a curse is a curse!'

'This is enough! We can't live like this, woman!' He strode out of the door and headed into the garage and stood for a moment looking at his pride and joy. The motorbike gleamed, black and silver, not the heap of scrap metal like it was sixteen years ago. He stroked the upholstered leather seat lovingly. He thought of the dream he had had of Carlotta riding pillion with him along the Highway and cruising round Bridgetown. But he had only taken it out once; Carlotta refused to go on it. He sat astride it, and rolled the handles lovingly beneath his palms. He turned the key, felt the roar between his thighs. He eased it out of the garage and along the driveway. Andreatta turned from the gate to look at him, reached her hand out and ran her fingers along the handlebars. Two motorcycle helmets hung there. Her large underwater eyes were wide with longing. She opened the gate for him and stepped aside. Their eyes met, and both turned to stare back at the house. She climbed on.

Carlotta ran out into the garden screaming her daughter's name. But she was too late; Marti was speeding down the road, heading for the Highway. Their daughter's head of curls sprung free beneath the helmet.

Carlotta fell onto the driveway, her hands over her face. She sat there, shoulders shaking, tears falling. The sun was warm on her back. She rose up.

The yard looked different. The bougainvillea sprawling on the picket fence seemed less bushy. The old mango tree suddenly looked young and green, the sunlight pouring through its leaves, the patio bright. A brisk breeze blew up and brisker still. It bent and broke the stems of the climbers hugging the wall, scattering petals across the yard like offerings for a Hindu festival. Carlotta watched in fascination as the clouds overhead went spinning past like those images of time-lapse photography. She headed for the veranda, sat down and waited.

As the sunset spread she heard the sound of the motorbike roaring down the street, slowing as it entered the yard. As she watched, her daughter dismounted, lifted the helmet and shook her newly cropped head free.

'Don't say a word, Mum,' she said. 'It'll grow back, if I let it. I decided it was time I took matters into my own hands.'

MOUTH

Mouth has to guard herself, zip up tight. Too much to lose. One slip and there's that image of her little granddaughter's face pressed up against the car window.

One slip and she's back there, in the petrol station, waiting, after all those months when she didn't know where little Flower was, where *they* were.

That wasn't the only time. After that came Eastbourne and the women's refuge. The policeman at the door calming her. Assuring her that this time they will get the Desperado, put him away. Effie will give evidence, yes. They've been waiting years to get that bastard.

Time for Sandra runs backwards, runs forwards. Sometimes she can't remember what happened first or after, only pockets of illuminated history that haunt her during the day, wake her at night.

She remembers Eastbourne, the long train journey, and there they were, Effie and Flower, waiting. She hadn't seen them for weeks. The day spent walking through the shopping centre, going to the beach. Effie making plans, a new start, go to college maybe. Flower's eyes shining with fear and tears, holding her granny's hand, missing her school, her friends. She was six years old. They would be relocated. Flower's arms are tight around Sandra's neck at the station. Back home Sandra is afraid to go out, afraid the friends of the Desperado are watching her from the darkness of their cars, waiting to follow her, see if she leads them to Effie.

Her lovely Effie, beautiful, flighty Effie.

Another snapshot: another refuge. The Desperado is with them and there are two more children. Sandra's heart is racing like a whippet in her chest, he's standing at the railway station with his smirky grin saying we've sorted it out, plus there's another baba on the way. Effie is beaming, she looks at him constantly, laughs at all his jokes. Then they are at a busy main road and the Desperado is strutting across bare-chested, his t-shirt swinging in one hand, uncaring of the traffic, expecting Effie and the pushchair and his children to follow. Sandra grabs their hands, makes them wait for the Green Man. They're in a park with dodgems and boat rides and his laugh is a moving carnival head spinning round and round as he recounts how he rides and falls off his motorbike at speed and doesn't care in the least if he falls, has broken every bone, is happy to see the blood and bruises, evidence that he was there. King of the road. And later Effie will whisper that he was traumatised by a father who stumped out his cigarettes on him and he can't help it if he's got no social graces, he's been in and out of Borstal since he was fourteen. And the policeman at Sandra's door is angry. Effie has compromised a police investigation, has compromised the secrecy and safety of a women's refuge.

When Effie was small Sandra used to tease her, call her Alice in Wonderland when she cried and cried over the smallest thing. Look, she would say, showing her Tenniel's drawing, the room of tears.

When mobiles came in, Sandra was over the moon. No more would she have to wait for telephone calls from phone boxes scattered round the country. A week or more going by, without word, the endless pacing in the front room looking at the phone. Trying to distract herself by cleaning all the rooms, stairs, kitchen. Pausing in Effie's old room, tidy now, ballet photos and trophies neat on the dresser. She stands in the front room looking out of the bay window. So many years looking out that window: from school times onward. Her face pressed up against the glass, worrying. Abduction, car accident. The relief when her daughter appeared round the corner and her own shoulders dropping, ready for whatever mood she was in this time. But the devil was waiting anyway, he ate school uniforms for breakfast, and nothing in all Sandra's fears would prepare her for his ascent to earth, and the spread of his black wings. After the baby and all that had happened, to keep close was her only aim. Keep close and look out for Flower.

Mobiles coming in ironically coincided with them settling. No more would she have to take the bus and worry all through the thirty-minute journey to the temporary accommodation. Walk through the Old Town and its beat-up houses, its boarded-up shops to the flat over a pub. On one of her visits, Sandra had heard and seen her daughter leaning out of the open sash window, exchanging banter with a group of men standing below. It was almost theatrical. The young Juliet with her Rapunzel hair. A cast of Capulets and Montagues. She sweated in her sandals when Effie spotted her and waved maniacally.

'Watch your language, guys, there's my mum!'

All eyes had swung to Sandra crossing the square, the Waitrose carrier bag knocking against her knees.

She never knew what she might find. That time her daughter was high, gabbling ten to the dozen as she found cups and made tea. But Flower was naked except for her nappy, her mouth smeared with chocolate, her bottle permanently attached to her lips. When Sandra questioned whether she was old enough to drink cow's milk, Effie had flipped, and the subsequent telephone call from the current social worker, that nice young man with the clean shaven face, had warned Sandra she needed to hold her tongue, keep the relationship going, trust Effie to make her own judgements.

Her daughter blew hot and cold as she always had. Non-communication was the weapon she used, and the weeks that went by with phone silence could be followed with Flower delivered by taxi, deposited at the door with her bottle and her teddy swinging from her hand. Sandra would never know how long she would stay, or where her mother was and in time Effie's room would become Flower's, and whilst she slept Sandra would look in on her and think it was Effie. They would just be getting into a routine when they would turn up to collect her, the Desperado's car pawing the road like a steed.

Effie got given a mobile the same time as she was given the little terrace by the railway station, and at first it was a novelty. The phone calls were frequent and full of joy. The Desperado, as Sandra had coined him, was always on the road somewhere, and Sandra had frequent missiles of hope in her tight chest as she met Effie for coffee or went round for lunch. There had been a moment she had wanted to do the right thing, take him to court for sex with a minor, but Effie had warned her to haul her neck in, or she would move away and Sandra would never see her or Flower again. She had never told the social workers who Flower's father was.

Mouth was becoming a stranger in her own country. Sentences could no longer flow. Each word had to be carefully chosen so as not to upset Effie. Sandra herself had had an uncomplicated childhood and had no idea that such complex people existed. The dance between her and Effie had been a tornado that began even as Effie screamed her way out of her and demanded the moon and the stars. She had loved her completely and instantly.

It is more difficult to accept darkness in the beautiful. At first she had tried to defer her daughter's restless energy, paid for countless years of dance lessons at which Effie was brilliant, but she didn't hold with the discipline. That went for school too, and Sandra still had nightmares where the devil was waiting outside with his Rover, revving his engine up again and again and again.

Mobiles could be turned off. And here is Sandra again, biliousness in her mouth as she walks up the long road by the railway station, a bag of fairy cakes in her hand. There is a baby seagull in the road. Flower's kitten is mewing outside the door, becoming more high pitched and plaintive as Sandra comes up the path. There's a gull screeching from the rooftop. She picks up the kitten instinctively. A free newspaper is stuck in the letterbox. Even as she retrieves it to bang the flap, she knows no one is there. There's no side entrance. She moves to the windows where the curtains hang loose and haphazardly half-open. The kitten purrs into her neck as she peers in. The sofa is upended, cushions strewn on the floor. Flower's high chair is lying on its side and two half-filled bin bags lean against each other on the carpet.

She can't remember how she got home with the cat. Maybe she called a taxi.

The police are not interested.

'Your daughter is an adult, she can do what she likes.'

'She's not an adult, she's 17.'

Silence.

'What address is it, please?'

'Well, we're not legally permitted to give details but I can confirm that we were called out to a disturbance at that address last Thursday.'

Mouth is a basket of fish on a jetty. They are jam-packed tight, breathing in the wet dew of their compressed selves. The gills of those at the top still move. They lift like the sails of a ship on a becalmed sea.

The Desperado parked his car at the Esso garage and there is Flower, her small face pressed against the glass, her eyes laden with tears.

'Granny!'

★★★

It's a small kitchen and the dog cage takes up a third of it. Sandra stops in the doorway. The dog is no longer the puppy she had last seen bounding round the living room. She remembered the kids running with her to the park, and them all settled like a wave on the sofa.

'What...?'

Effie is close behind her, words tumbling.

'She's driving me mad, Mum, wrecking the place and chewing the kids' toys and pooing everywhere! I can't have it with the baby! Plus that bastard doesn't like dogs.'

'But...'

'I know I KNOW!' She holds her hands up and pushes

past Sandra to get at the kettle. 'Don't say I told you so! I just wanted something for ME!'

'You can't keep a dog like this in a cage, it's not fair!'

'Well, life's not fair is it!'

The dog had recognised Sandra, and lifted her doleful eyes at her. Her tail began a slow wag.

'Don't let her con you, she's been fed.'

The sink is piled high with dishes and Sandra watches as her daughter digs out two mugs and washes them.

'How much time does she spend in here?'

'Only a couple of hours. When the kids come home Mikey will take her for a walk.'

'Why don't you let her out into the garden?'

'For Chrissake! You haven't seen me for two months and all you can do is ask after the stupid dog?! What about me?'

'You never answer your phone, Effie, and it's not easy for me to come halfway round the country!'

Sandra crossed to the kitchen door and pushed it open.

A pile of dog mess waits on the path.

Arms and legs of dolls protrude through the long grass like dismembered soldiers.

The trampoline takes up half the garden. The ring of grass beneath it is dead, a graveyard of broken toys and plastic cups, a muddied blanket.

Mouth is a corral of wild horses. They buck and prance in a carnival of frenzy, filling the air with dust and stones.

Sandra remembers the telephone call just two months ago, her daughter's happy voice mobiling its way out of Wilkinson, the plants, she said, going for a song.

'What happened to your vegetable garden?'

Effie was behind her with the tea.

'She ruined it, stupid dog. And the kids. Dug up everything I planted. I had peas and everything. Look...' she pointed to the border by the fence, busy with dandelions and a hogweed, its lacy head anointing the dark fence like a parasol.

On the train home, she can't stop thinking about the dog. Contemplates calling the RSPCA. Pretend to be anonymous. But how could you do that to your own daughter? The faces of the children rise up before her.

Her mouth is growing tired of keeping secrets, shape-shifting, deflecting well-meaning queries about Effie, the children, five of them now, five.

★★★

There's a broken window in the bay, replaced with cardboard. Sandra rings the bell and Chrissie opens the door, swinging on the handle. The children's heads appeared in the dark doorway like vines. No, sunflowers. Those beaming faces. Sandra tries not to show her surprise; it's a school day.

She stumbles in the wake of the children, the pushchairs and scattered shoes.

Effie is lying on the sofa feeding the baby. She moves to lower the volume of the TV with the remote.

'Hello, Mum.'

Sandra tries to look past the paraphernalia of toys and shoes and scattered clothes, the used nappy on the coffee table, the high chair with the remains of spaghetti hoops, the cat asleep on the dining table. The college application lies heavy in her bag.

'You're looking well,' Mouth said brightly. 'Everything ok?'

'Yeah, yeah,' Effie yawned. 'Just woken up. This little madam kept me up all night. We all had a lay in, didn't we kids?'

'Yay!' they all shouted, settling into the sofa and grabbing the remote.

'Where's Flower?' Sandra asked.

'That madam! Still in bed I guess.'

She passed the baby to Sandra and shifted off the sofa. Sandra spied the bruise on her thigh before Effie swiftly pulled her dressing gown down.

'Coffee?'

'Look what Daddy did to the window, Granny!' Chrissie said.

***

Sandra inched her way down the steps with yet another black bag. Effie passed her on the way, her arms full of washing, phone in hand. She'd spent all morning trying to sort out her benefits.

'Thanks, Mum, I don't know what I'd do without you.'

Which house was this? It wasn't the terrace. That was long gone. Might have been the one by the harbour. Where they had the staffie and a tiny courtyard which Sandra tried to make nice for Effie, with coloured slate and palms from Homebase. But then there was dog crap everywhere and fleas in the carpet.

Mouth is an auditorium filled to the rafters with sighs.

***

She and Flower are riding the bus, looking forward to the

weekend. Why did she say, 'Flower, it looks like Mum can't cope. The place is so untidy. Can you help her a bit more?' Kids love their parents no matter what. It might have been like that game of Chinese Whispers. Flower might have had a row with her mum and said, 'Granny said this place is messy!' Effie was on the phone quicktime. 'How dare you say my house is disgusting! I'm fed up with people looking down on me. You'll never see your grandchildren again!'

How many months had it been that time? Unanswered text messages, changed numbers, letters returned ripped inside their Return to Sender envelopes. Mouth had swallowed and swallowed her pain. The words that kept coming up like vomit made their way back down her throat. Then came the time the Law finally got their man. Maybe the drug scene was overcrowded with dealers; maybe he needed easy and instant money. Whatever. The Desperado was caught red-handed in a forklift truck smashing an ATM.

There were two years then, of relative peace. Kids over for the weekend. Lunches out. Flower started piano which Sandra paid for. Little ones started school, though many times they were late. Effie never was good at waking up. Mikey did what he always did, spent hours in his room playing video games that had 18 on the cover. Lots of people make mistakes, Sandra would say, tentatively. Here's a chance, start over. She brought the college brochures out of her bag. But then came Desperado number 2 and then Desperado number 3 who lined the kitchen worktop with vodka bottles. Smashers of windows and mobile phones. Visits to the prison for confused children. And then the return of Desperado 1 and the time he used the landline and Sandra picked up. *Hi, Sand, your alright? Get that nutty daughter of yours willya.* And Mouth broke without thinking. *How dare you speak to me like that?* And his laugh dropped like pellets down the phone, *Lighten up, Sand, itz only Bipolar innit!*

Sandra had dropped the phone like a hot pan, his words thrusting into the room like lasers. How could she not have known? How could she not have known? Jesus. Her own daughter. Oh Jesus. She had sunk down onto the sofa frozen, and even when Effie came bounding down to answer the phone, she was still frozen, her mouth slack with fear.

★★★

Sandra slinks down in horror and exhaustion against the bedroom wall. She is shaking. The voices of the landlord and his wife are still ringing in her ears. She should have been prepared for this. Why else would Effie have wandered off with the first vanload to the new house? She had bluffed her way using the children as an excuse, *get them out of the way.* The new garden was huge and just right for children, with a rope-swing and a treehouse. And at last, a room for each of the children. *You can manage here, Mum, can't you? You and Pete?*

Sandra had stared at the chaos around them in shock. Nothing had been prepared. The only word that she could conjure was *Tsunami.*

It looks worse than it is, Effie had said unconvincingly. *Once the big things go it's only the black bags and the boxes, I've been packing for weeks.* Sandra's mouth had opened like a crocodile and then snapped shut.

Whilst Pete began to lift the furniture into the hired van

with Desperado Number 3, Sandra had made her way upstairs. She had stood at the doorway of the boys' room and shook her head. Broken beds. Clothes rail weighed down with clothes. Large TV. Toys. Black bags.

Flower's room was no different.

With the bed gone the carpet was alive with *things*. Barbies. Coke bottles. Crisp packets.

You can't blame the kids. They haven't been taught. It's the throwaway society, Sandra, remember.

There was a banging at the front door. Everyone had gone off with the van. Sandra made her way downstairs.

'So it's true she's doing an effing runner?!'

A large man in a leather jacket stood in the doorway. He barged past Sandra, followed by a small woman with her arms crossed.

Over and over, for the next three hours, as she sorted the unusable, the litter, the for-charity and the useful, Sandra played and replayed the scene. The landlord. His wife. Effie not informing them. Effie not paying the rent. Effie ruining their pension fund. The rotted laminate floor where the rabbits and the dog had peed and pooed. Broken kitchen cupboards. The smashed window. The shower minus door. On and on. They walked in and out of rooms shaking their heads. The woman was in tears. Sandra followed them like a ghost, in shame, seeing through someone else's eyes all that she had swallowed, internalised, commented on, tried to fix, careful not to upset Effie. Her loyalty and love for her broken, delusional daughter wavering at the edge of her mouth. I've tried, she says lamely, all her life I've tried.

She catches sight of herself in a mirror still hanging on the wall. Sees herself now, small and broken, leaning against a wall lined with black sacks. All those unspoken words are festering in the swirl of her throat. She is ashamed that she did not do anything about the dog. She is ashamed she didn't do anything about the rabbits. She is ashamed she didn't do anything about the children apart from bring them sweets and bid them work hard at school. She is negating the worn tread of her shoes up the paths of all those houses, hates herself for not doing what she should have done all those years ago, report the Desperado for sexual acts with a minor. All those threats about not seeing her daughter and grandchildren had nevertheless come true, because they did not see her in a clear light. They saw her as part of this crazy deal called life, her silence an ally for the mother they loved and depended on but knowing, as they grew, that there was something not quite right. Most of all she is ashamed she didn't recognise what her daughter needed from way, way back.

She knows now what she has to do. Knows if she doesn't it will go on and on still. Reaching for her mobile, she hears a strange sound, coming, it seemed, from a long way off, her voice: a plaintive, wailing escalation of a creature in distress.

SUGARCANE FOR MY SWEETHEART

Maya is dreaming of kitchens. New kitchens. Not open to the air, wood-smoke kitchens; not kerosene stoves or coal-pot kitchens. New kitchens. Kitchens of pine and oak and beech. Kitchens with solid wood doors and MDF shelves, kitchens with laminate and chrome, Mediterranean tiles, Victorian pulleys, cork and slate floors, quarry tiles.

In her dreams she enters those kitchens as she has taken to entering all those showrooms on lunchtime Sundays: with the slow excited steps of a traveller arriving. Eyes stray past Customs, the loitering salesman, the swing doors past Immigration. Gleaming glass-fronted doors hold her gaze like shimmering tarmac. They draw her in like mirrors, framing the new arrival. Excitement is mixed with fear and longing, slowed by the shuffling progress of the queue.

Her kitchen measurements are clutched tight in her hands like a passport; over and over she checks them: the permit, the invitation letter, traveller's cheques crisp and new in their plastic sleeve.

She has reason to feel afraid. On her return from the island the eyes of the officer had scalded Maya. They highlighted her like a spotlight, running her up and down as if they could see right through her. A chorus had risen from the queue like the tide, washing over her with a high Atlantic wave. In this dream her mother is by her side, her spirit hands even more frantic in death, fluttering a British passport that only Maya could see, tickets and boarding passes scattering on the desk like the plucked feathers of a broiling bird.

In her dream the showrooms stretch: long corridors of gleaming perfection. Miles and miles of shining flooring glide her on its conveyor belt, kitchen after kitchen smiling like models, preening their leaded light and bubble-glassed doors, their plaited cornices like wooden pigtails, their panels in Bermuda Blue, Nevada Blond, Pine Forest. Her dreams have kept up with fashion, solid pine and farmhouse oak that had once beamed their rustic Englishness, Middle England Agas nestling securely like the Cotswold Hills, no longer feature. Now chrome and beech and Shaker kitchens lure her, will her to run her fingers on their smooth fine grain, their granite and Corian worktops combining style and utilitarian twenty-first century designs.

The salesman disappears. Other dreamers have re-commissioned him; they sit in the conservatory-style office with their dream kitchen coming alive on a computer screen, Mr and Mrs Doggy nodding, car-window heads beaming. Their Cheshire smiles fill Maya's vision and suddenly she is horizontal, being whisked along white corridors with ceilings of ceramic hobs, their halogen spotlights steaming her face like Granny's Vicks. Perspiration is running down her cheeks, the small of her back. The steward has opened the aircraft door and Maya is descending. Heat washes over her like invisible rain. Tarmac ripples in the haze. The redcap boys run with their luggage trolleys. Water runs down her back. She is a dog in the shadows, turning over and over in the liquid heat, an insistent voice riding over the surf.

'Maya! Maya!'

Denver is nuzzling his face into her neck. His hand rests on her hip. Her eyes flutter into a still-dark morning. She senses his body wakening. He is not yet, fully. In a minute he will be, and remember. He'll turn away then, face his own wall, summon the energy to rise, get ready for work.

Beneath her the towel is damp and hard. Many washes in this limescaled water has wrung any softness out. She thinks of the towels in Uncle Danny's bathroom, the white fleshy softness, her body cosseted, white tiles reflecting her face. There was no limescale back there. How she loved to hang the washing out then! Hook them on the line, watch them dance like kites in the wild wind, sing in a soft breeze. She had washed everything in sight, tea cloths, Uncle Danny's clothes, her own. Just to smell them, feel them, watch them dry face up to the sun, unaccustomed in cold dank London.

The first thing they tell you when you return is to tek it easy, you back home now. So fill your eyes with the coconut trees, the endless beach, the boats turning out to sea. Lone fishermen pushed their bikes across the sand, their dogs nosing alongside. And the sky, the sky! That brilliant cobalt blue, stretching a panorama between memory and reality. Tourists didn't make it this far. Here it was too rough to swim, the waves still angry at history, guarding the wrecks viciously. Their anger had moved from scuttles to schooners and jet skis, to slippery fishing boats with secret cargoes. And you try and take it easy. Borrow that inherent ambiance, live one day at a time. But soon you realise that what you're doing is waiting. Waiting for time to stand still. Time has stood still for Maya in this particular place.

Waiting. Watching the shifting blues, the white haze, the fisherman becoming a dot. The clothes on the line have dried, her swimsuit a kitten at play, relishing this now-time, this brief sojourn before being folded into a drawer, nestling in the dark like a hyacinth bulb.

Maya is always dreaming. Maya has always dreamt. 'What stories!' Her mother had laughed, woken by Maya crying about the cane-man. 'There are no cane-fields here, you silly child. Here, drink some sugar-water, it will calm you down.'

Maya dreams of children. Tall, brown-skinned children, running in from the sun asking for limeade with ice, American Kool-Ade, coconut water cold from the fridge. Even now, even now, with no longer the slightest chance that such a thing would ever happen, she still dreamed of herself waiting to welcome them home from school, running into a clean house with the floor swept and polished, washing clean on the line, and in the kitchen, the up-to date modern kitchen, corn-pone and coconut cake smelling succulent and sweet right up to the eaves.

The first thing she had done after the operation, on the first clear day without drugs when the sharp pain had dulled, was to slide her fingers down there, checking to see if the stories were true. Her hand had bypassed her tender stomach with its new wound, slipped into softness, parting, investigating. So many horror stories: of surgeons' knives slipping, cutting the nerves. Of women losing all sensation there. The night ward had been alive with women tossing in their sleep, nurses prowling, whispers. She had felt so guilty. She heard her mother's voice screaming, 'Maya! What you got your hand in you panty for, you nasty girl!' But she had to know. Her mind had jumped to Denver, his mouth running down her smooth belly. 'That's what I love about you, baby, you're always so ready for me.' He could slide into her anytime, day or night. 'Like a canoe through mangroves,' he had whispered. Only Maya knew the real truth, that this was the only place she could not submerge, could not guard, could not disguise.

Everything else, she could have told him, was in disguise. The way she moved, spoke, borrowed a terrestrial space she did not own, was not hers. But touch her there, and she woke, jumped to the touch, indeed, never slept; like the washing on the line, somersaulting with immeasurable abandon.

He props himself up on one elbow, looking down at her. She can't look at him; her eyes seek focus on the Gauguin print, on the drape of the mosquito net, bought for style, not purpose.

'I didn't know this was going to happen,' he says.

She tries to answer but the words don't know what shape to take. She is out in mid-Atlantic somewhere, flirting with the steward, feeling like an astronaut might do when re-entering the atmosphere. The Caribbean accent is like whale-song, swimming deep inside her, rippling in veins, bubbling in corpuscles. *Yuh would like to try the pan-fry chicken?* The voice and the sexual banter count as a package. For the first time Maya thought about herself as a package purely dependent on hormones. About nuance, verbal foreplay, legs criss-crossing on a barstool. The teasing smile on a stranger's lips when glances dance between you even when you both know it ain't going nowhere, but is lava of life while it's bubbling. For the first time, on that airplane seat, Maya start to frighten that her smiling time it done. That she ain't got nothing to promise no more.

'Fresh fruit, vitamins, oily fish,'

The doctor only glances at her briefly, eyes glued to his computer screen where 'D'Andrade, Maya', heads a page listing Miscarriages 5, Hysterectomy, (recent), and Post-Menopausal Depression now being typed in.

He slides a prescription form for anti-depression pills towards her.

'We can't recommend HRT in your case, so this is the only way forward.'

Maya leaves the surgery, walks along North Road on a cold November day. Enters the house she shares with Denver, the dark cheerless kitchen, and lines the tablets up on the worktop. Speaks to them:

I an know how fa start telling Denver these things. Is not easy like pulling up a chair and saying, Denver man, some things are happening bodywise that making things a bit difficult. On the whole my Denver is an understanding man. What other man would let his woman recuperate in the Caribbean? Swan off, ketch a plane, siddown on Uncle Danny veranda for six whole weeks. And come to that, what kinda women in her right mind would want to step back to that 'nother country? That 'nother country of sugarcane and heat?

Maya knew there was plenty she put to the back of she mind. Denver think he know her. Love she for ten years, hold her hand through every baby lost.

It was Denver who had stolen her call-name, re-christened her his Sugarcane Baby, forced her into his crotch through love-play. 'My own piece of Caribbean ass,' he would grunt, lured as much by her history as by her. How she gon tell Denver he sugarcane baby now dry up like cane-trash?

She did never see Denver so vex with her in all she life. Is 'no', she say, 'no'. He did fling the tickets them right across the room. Ranting and raving that all the time she does talk about back-home, all the times she moaning how England hard and cold, now when she have an opportunity to go home is no she say, no.

'I don't know what you want, girl, I can't help you. You gotto help you own self now. Don't even ask where I get the money! And you know how much trouble it take to find you mother brother? How much time I spend going through your mother things what you lock up in the attic? I thought this would be a surprise! And look at the thanks I get!'

She had had no choice but to go. Re-enter that world she had left as a child. Walk down those roads. Remember them dogs coupling in the backyard? Stuck together, back to back for hours sometimes, tongues hanging out in the heat? The neighbours would fetch water, throw. Chase them out the yard and down the road still lock together, the bitch yelping. Maya did yelp once too, but nobody din hear her.

Maya dreaming 'bout sugarcane. She dreaming she out on a farm road, the heat rolling ahead of her like waves.

A man is pushing a cart by hand, no donkey, no tractor. The cart is pile up high with fresh cut cane, green and shining, their limbs hanging down sad over the cartwheel. The man cutlass is hanging down too, strap to his trousers by a piece of nylon rope. Maya get frighten because she on her own on this road and she know the man can do what he want, is she one waiting on this lonesome road. Then the man stop he cart close by Maya trembling self and throw she such a sweet smile Maya cry with the sweetness of it.

His smile belying his actions because at the same time his hands reaching to pluck that cutlass from his makeshift belt and slice through the air so fast that she dint have time to know what happening till that piece of sugarcane is lying in her hand. And suck she remember to suck, even though in the dream Maya know is a dream and is years since she suck sugarcane. But she suck and suck cos she thirsty and the man disappearing down the road. Suck till is only the stalk lef, fibre, dry like string. From nowhere, as is the style of dreams, water come; and Maya looking in a pool and know why the man dint bother her. For this wasn't Maya true self staring back at her but some old crone with a mash-up face and naked gums. Again she wake up wet and crying.

Uncle Danny, when he step out on the veranda, is a old man. His mouth mash up, he got no teeth. He has shrunk too. His grey eyes are opaque in his walnut skin, crinkled at the edges from years of squinting at the sun. He entertains her with local gossip, the fishing boat caught just last week with thousands of dollars worth of marijuana, the oil spill, the Williams boy back from Toronto building a house. Then he falls into his old man routine, nods off halfway through an anecdote. Sleeps, eats, rests. Not once in all those weeks is he anything but an old man, breathing in the pattern of sleep and wake, stumbling intermittently round the frizzled vegetable patch. Only when time comes for her to leave and the hire car waiting, does he place his skeletal arms around her and press something in her hand. A piece of fresh sugarcane. The season coming to a end now, his says, through pink gums.

The season coming to an end. Maya dreaming of kitchens. Bright clean kitchens with smooth gleaming worktops. There are windows everywhere and electric light shining. When the sweats wake her she rises, and begins to clean.

She scrubs the walls, the floor, each corner where the shadows linger. She sprays ant killer in every crevice where a cockroach or centipede might hide. She rinses Denver's lunch box out from the bleach soak and makes him sandwiches without crusts, in perfect triangles. If Denver rises, and tries to put his arm around her, she becomes wild, screaming, 'Y'all dirty dawgs, hise yuh tails outa here! Now ah gon have to clean this whole blasted place again before the children come home from school!

'Is children season', she sings, as she cleans, 'is children season.'

WRITING ON WATER

Dolly would have made a thing of it. Would have flown into the airport dolled up to the nines or rode into town on the back of a cattle-truck after thumbing her way from Rosslaire wearing the cut-off jeans and the biker jacket. No one would have dared hijack her, harass her, or not give her a ride. She would have had that Caribbean lip curled ripe and ready. She would have had lodgings right in town, last-minute, even in this busiest of weeks in this small town now waking up to its annual invasion of writers. Her appearance at Reception in The Irish Arms would have occasioned wide white smiles of recognition, and ripples would have oscillated round the bar as her butt found either a barstool or the wing of a leatherette armchair.

'Of course, Miss Dolly! Room 19 has just become available. Room Service?'

Dolly wasn't afraid of anything, land, sea or sky.

But this wasn't Dolly, this was Marlee, and try as hard as she might to summon her, Dolly would not put in an appearance. Instead the black-cloud child was driven sullen but safely into town in the beat-up old Escort with hubby Daniel at the wheel.

Boats and planes filled her with fear. She was the dreamwalker, the pre-planner who endlessly negotiated N routes and B roads, small village main streets and country crossroads with no placenames, for fourteen hours, rather than come on her own, or fly. And of course, the self-catering was five miles out of town.

Before she even crossed that damn water, things had gone wrong. They arrived at Fishguard in driving wind and rain to find the ferry cancelled. Her damp heart and low spirits had never lifted, not even with the promise of an extra day in Pembrokeshire. But then the sun had come out, and they'd gone climbing the cliffs; or rather Dan had and she followed, him cheery as usual, pointing out the benefit of an extra day at no cost.

But of course there was cost, there always was. Sixty-five quid at The Ferryman's Inn, cutting into their holiday money, leaving them (as usual) to count coppers and pence and, this time, euros. For Marlee, sixty-five had a kind of ring to it; the number of loss.

It was Dolly who had opened her big mouth about wanting to write a novel. I'm going to try a novel, she had declared. Poetry doesn't pay, no one wants it. A whopping yarn, lots of sex, and tragedy, beautiful people, maybe the fashion world! She had all the ideas: they floated round in her head all the time like moons and stars, circling.

It was Dolly who came up with all the beautiful lines in the useless poetry. She had names and places, family stories from way back that were too true to ever be fiction; sugar plantations, lost wives, even murder. All she needed was a kick-start. Novelists had to do it different from poets or else poets would be rich too. Would be swimming in advances and film rights, wouldn't have time to feel as sick as a toddler every time they had to catch a flight or a ferry. They lived in places like Welsh mountainsides and sat in proper studies with proper computers and did research, writing consistently each day in between annoying telephone calls from their editors demanding they see the manuscript right now, this minute, this weekend, the final deadline or they would cull the next advance immediately. Dolly had no patience with small terraced houses and no night life. She insisted she was a South American woman, Caribbean *and* Black British *and* Citizen of the World. Marlee had listened her out, thinking of all the open mics she did, the odd poem accepted in a magazine, the small class she taught; cast her eye at the dining table and the laptop she shared with Dan. Think big, Dolly had yawned, you silly little shore-bird.

That had settled it; a novel-writing workshop it would be.

That was why she had not, could not enjoy the unforeseen and unplanned day in Pembrokeshire. She had business to be getting on with, and the Irish Sea was the first of her hurdles. She hadn't bargained on coastal paths too. But she'd waited in her walking boots by the car as Dan fidgeted about with binoculars and raincoats, rucksacks, the first-aid box. The Englishness of it never failed to stump her; as a child, walking was strolling, window-shopping, or taking the breeze; no one in their right minds walked precipitous miles for pleasure. Bacoo would get you, jiggers and thief-man choke and rob; obeah, fever, sun.

She'd followed him out to the lighthouse, hugging the cliff, crossing stiles, liking the sun on her back. But she kept an eye out for nutters. You could never tell. There was no telling her not to worry, things happened; like that poor couple last year, robbed, washed up on the rocks. She'd tried to block worry out, turn her face to the sun, breathe in audibly like Dan, hands on hips, binoculars at the ready. Focused on the black-backed gulls and cormorants and

Christ knows whatever else bobbing out there. But when it came to scrambling up a tilting path with nothing to grab on to but a steady tread and a trusting heart, she'd bottled out. Sat firmly on the flattest rock with her face turned away from the jeering sea and steadied her gaze onto one solitary pissed-off sheep. No amount of persuading would shift her, no kindness, no practice run by Dan down the track backwards to show how easy it was. So back down they had gone, passing nimble children on the way up in trainers and women in sandals all happy and smiling like idiots. One even had a blade of grass in her teeth.

But then they'd seen the seals, and that had saved the day, rinsing out her worries in a bright pink watercolour haze to be plucked out from memory when they were sitting in the Roseland Retirement Home. She'd been sure one of the seals was dead. It hadn't moved all the time they watched. Just lay with its head back, chest up to the sky.

'Just basking,' Dan had informed her.

Of course the sea was rough. It had to be. Their wait on the dockside had been alight with raucous Munster fans re-enacting a victory over Wales at Cardiff. One, pissed as a fart, cornered her by the ladies toilets and asked her if she had any idea where da boat was. Faced with more of the same for four hours on an uptight sea, they had blown twenty-five quid on a cabin, and for all the hours bumped up against each other whilst the sea rolled like a tumbledee.

Her mind had been alive with blackness. The black rocks of Pembrokeshire had followed the ferry, creeping with the delicacy of giants along the floor of the Irish Sea. They offered her cinematic visions of *The Herald of Free Enterprise*, French Napoleonic Fleets, an English galleon filled with merchants and soldiers and a Captain who looked remarkably like Charles Hawtrey, dangling a small black boy on a chain.

'I can't wait to see you guys again!' Dolly had told Marie on the phone. Images of Listowel during Writers' Week danced around in her head. Earnest authors and passionate poets, singing pubs and leather upholstery, the Lakes of Killarney. 'I love y'all country so much! Can't wait to get there!'

'We can't wait to see you too, girl!'

So here she was, in Ireland.

The workshop she wanted was full. Everyone, it seemed, wanted to write novels.

'There's a place on the poetry,' the smiley woman said.

'I don't want to do poetry,' Marlee said. 'I am a poet. I don't need to do a poetry workshop! I run them myself, for God's sake. Poetry is my shadow; it wakes me up in the middle of the night. I've reams and reams of the useless stuff. I'm tired of introspection and internal torment, do you get me, woman? Tired!

'I want to write a fecking novel. Something big and grand that'll get me noticed and buy me a ranch in California and a place on the bookshelves of Waterstones. I want to sign books in the marquee at Dartington!'

She felt she was waving her arms about madly as she spoke, but of course she wasn't. She never said a word. Just stood there her usual sullen self and said, 'I guess that'll have to do then.'

Behind her Dolly sucked her teeth, loudly, and full of disgust.

There was, she had to admit, something quite cool about

meeting her Irish friends in their Irish town and going to a writing workshop during an Irish Festival. A good tutor too, the best. She taught his work in her Creative Writing class, could quote his poetry off by heart. And if she wanted to enjoy this second-home feeling, there was no place else that would give it her. The other writers were from the length and breadth of Ireland, even a property developer from Dublin.

Her post-colonial profile fitted in just right.

The writers were all at varying stages, from first-time to published, from the too-busy-to-write to the waiting-for-inspiration brigade. If she wanted to know Ireland, here is where it started, with her peers and all their Irishness to be drunk up. She wasn't just a holidaymaker, she was a Writer. She remembered the first time she had put *Writer* instead of *housewife* in her passport, that time they went to St Lucia. Dan was the only one who had spoilt things there, hob-nobbing with the sailors on the pretend-pirate ship, fist-shakes the lot. *You're just a tourist to them*, she had told him coldly. *Just like I'm a 'Red Girl'*.

Yes, she was a griot, history had given her this pen dammit, she never asked. Seamus, Walcott, there ya go. She felt herself warming, enjoying, taking part. The group had bonded by coffee-time but by lunch the gremlin was on her shoulder again.

Here you go again, Dolly said, you silly bitch. Poetry's reeling you in like a marlin! That's you sorted then, fish-bones on a bloody plate.

She paused at the bottom of the stairs and read details of the other workshops. Dammit, she had to stick to her plans. Novelists were different from poets, were more manly about things; faint heart never won fair maid and all that. She mustn't forget she was a whole-country woman, come a long way from de backdam. Whuh she grandmother with she calabash would think, eh?

She bit her lip and plucked up the courage, found the tutor she wanted, asked.

'Sure, and that's fine,' the tutor said. 'We're one short anyway.'

So why did she feel like shit?

'It's not you, it's me,' she told the Poet tutor lamely. 'I just wanted to try a Novel, that's all.'

She felt like a hick lover. His troubled poet-soul searched her eyes for the truth. But maybe she was only being fanciful.

She met the girls in The Irish Arms for a stew and large glasses of red wine.

'You did what?! Never! You bloody didn't. By Christ you're a woman you are! And so, how's the new one like?'

Dolly sang out: 'Full o' rass, we jus reading one heap o' stupidness after another.'

'So hang on, girl, let's get this right – you don't like this one either! For feck's sake!!'

Kristy leaned over the table and pointed her cigarette at Marlee.

'You know what you are, dontcha? A fecking workshop groupie!'

She and Marie fell about laughing.

'She looks the type, right Kirst? With the hair and all!'

'What I want to know is, where you going next?!'

Marlee found herself laughing along but lost the joke halfway. The Poet came into the bar and she tried to smile but he wouldn't catch her eye.

She and Dan lay in bed at the self-catering. The rain was

drawing to a trickle. When she sat up, the fields crawled low and hazy under the belly of the horses.

'What's it like out there?'

'Shit,' she replied.

He opened his eyes.

'You're a cheery one, first thing. What's up?'

She was tired of hearing him ask what's up. Hadn't he realised yet that the all-singing all-dancing Dolly he had met in the wine bar all those years back wasn't real? The girls hadn't yet, she was sure. They thought her a badass Caribbean post-col sister with the bledy English History in common and an awright poet too. But they didn't have to wake up with her or sleep with her and her tossing and turning and dreaming of ships weighed down sailing for islands with black boys on the ocean. She felt sure they caught planes and ships only glad they hadn't missed them.

'Shouldn't you be getting ready for your workshop?'

'I'm not going.'

'What?'

'I don't want to talk about it,' she said briskly and clambered out of bed.

'But you've paid for it! Besides you've got the one you wanted haven't you?'

She couldn't explain. Just knew how bad she felt about the whole thing and wanted to tune into her feelings, follow her mind, like her mother always said.

'Let's go to Dingle, Kells Bay. Let's drive round the Ring of Kerry!'

'It's not exactly the day for it, is it?'

'For Chrissake! Are we on fucking holiday or not? Sod the weather, doesn't it always rain? We've only got a few days, let's make the most of it!'

'But I thought you...'

'Never mind what you think I thought. Get out of bed. Let's go.'

They hadn't chosen a good day. A famous writer had died and the town was out, cars and people gathered full in the square and right up to the church. There was TV and all. Marlee turned her head as the Guards waved their Escort on. For a hard moment she burned to stop and stand outside the church too. This was history. But, what is the point, Daniel said. There's nowhere to park plus I thought you wanted to do The Ring of Kerry.

The rain had cleared by the time they drove out of Tralee and bright sunshine accompanied the drive.

Before she knew it, her own clouds lifted. Like so many before them, they stopped at the beauty spots, struck by the sea and the light, the mountains. At what point did she begin to think of nature as beautiful? Never, in her childhood, with mosquitoes and the burning sun and no-go areas where, she was told, 'our sort of people don't wander'.

At Kells Bay, there was a house for sale, a white fisherman's cottage just up from the beach. Her heart was full in her chest as they drove round the crescent of the bay, and their conversation ran on house prices and writing spaces and the sea and its apparent tranquillity. Lies, Dolly whispered beneath her breath, you and I both know the truth about the sea.

At the Coomakista Viewing Point, Dan stopped and got out with his binoculars. The clouds were spinning fast like in those speeded-up films. Marlee thought about the dead writer and the people lining up in the street. And the burning dark eyes of the poet in the bar. Were they all bloody tormented then? Her heart slowed at the thought. She thought of the land she was born in floating away, and the words following it, stirring up their phrases like foam. Who was she to think the word 'home' meant a place? This ... in-between-ness, this was *it*.

Herein dwell the life she be. Without thinking she reached in her bag, pulled out her notebook and begun to write. From somewhere the words of Pablo Neruda came,

And it was at that moment Poetry arrived in search of me...

The words spilled from her pen as if they were writing themselves. Her own words *...arrived like a new Yamaha spilling dust and stones/up from the unpaved road...*

By the time Dan returned, flush-faced and windswept, she had the bones of a new poem.

It's no good, she thought. These are the stones that link me to the causeway. The words came like breakers over the shore, the Caribbean and Ireland, her loss in 1965; the migrant soul, poetry the unifying element. She could dream of a destination, a safe place, as long as she liked, be it the ranch in California, the Welsh mountain, a piece of Ireland. But none of it would fill her. Neither sleep, nor dreams, cliff paths, nor ships would anchor her. Her stomach was a cargo hold where the black boy would sing and sing until his throat was sore; whilst Dan snored and dreamed of oystercatchers. She wrote her name at the end of the poem. Dorothy Marley. Dorothy Marley.

TELLING BARBIE

Keep still; let me brush your hair. There, now you look beautiful. You have to look beautiful. Everyone tells me I'm beautiful. They've been saying it since I was small. People keep staring at me. They go on about my eyes and some stroke my hair. 'She's so beautiful,' they say. It's so annoying.

Mum is beautiful; everyone says I look like her. 'It's not all it's cracked up to be,' she says. Sometimes when she's cross she puts lipstick on and then rubs it off again.

I'm going to be Snow White at the party. I showed you my dress Mum got me from Asda, didn't I? It's blue and silky and has white frilly bits at the top and the bottom. I'm going to wear my slip-on party shoes and a tiara in my hair. My hair's getting really long isn't it? How do you think I'd look with short hair? Did your hair used to be long before...? Freda's going as Rapunzel. She looks like Rapunzel, don't she? Her hair is ginger like her dad. Only I'm not supposed to say ginger so Mum calls it straw blonde. Freda's dad is coming to the party, all our dads are. Except *Him* of course. I'm going to ask Mum if we can get you a Snow White dress too. You can't wear this old thing.

Mum's going as Cinderella, not Cinderella before she meets her godmother, Cinderella after she meets her godmother, when she waves her wand and her raggedy dress gets turned into a ballgown and the glass shoes and the pumpkin and everything. Mum doesn't want to look like Cinders, she said, bad enough her name is Ella. She asked me to pass her the ashtray when she was saying it and said that her whole life she's been bleeding Cinders and she's going to show those effing sisters of hers that she's getting her life together and they can just eff off. But she did ask them to the party.

I said to Mum I said, 'Why don't you be someone really different like Princess Fiona in *Shrek?*' And she looked at me and rolled her eyes and the phone started ringing and Davey started crying again and she shouted at me to pick him up the same time she shouted at Freda not to touch the bloody phone so I don't know what else she was going to say. I wanted to say that Tony looked like Shrek but I daren't.

Davey will be one years old when we have the party. That's not the only reason we're having it; it's the, it's the ... impetus, I think Mum said. It's a party for all of us and especially for Mum and Tony as sometimes he goes back to his mum. Mum told him last week he's a spoilt brat and he should have known what he was taking on board.

My dad is coming to the party. I don't think he likes Tony but Mum says it's about time everyone got on or she'll give them all what for.

I like my dad. Or at least I think I do. I didn't always like him. I haven't really known him all that long. Did you know him then? Mum says she kept you always even if you were in a black bag. She was always moving but she says she wants to stay here now. I was a baby when Dad went away and was at school when he came back. Freda's dad was living with us then. That was before *Him*. I like it when Dad picks me and Georgie up and we climb in his big dragon car with the dark windows and the engine coughing out lots of smoke. I'm glad he hasn't got that stupid van no more, the one where he piles us all in the back with not even any seats! I like it when he speeds up just as the lights turn red and slows down at green and he turns and looks at us laughing and pretends he's taking his hands off the wheel. I really scream! Georgie pretends he isn't scared, and he pushes his sunglasses up like Dad but I can see his fingers holding on really tight on the door-handle. And I like it as well when we roar into the drive-thru McDonald's and when we go go-kart racing. But I don't like it when we're staying over and Dad drops us at his girlfriend's. Melissa doesn't like me. She says to Dad, she says, 'haven't I got enough to do with my own kids?' She's got Becky and Donna but only Donna's my real sister. That's why I don't take you because they might take you away to make me talk.

Your feet are so dirty; I'm going to have to put you in the bath with Davey. Aw, since Sofie left I'm so busy helping Mum I don't get so much time to play with you. If I can find my Little Mermaid tea set we'll have tea and biscuits, or jammy dodgers. See if I can scrape off that nail polish on your toes. When Sofie was here I didn't have to do Davey's bottles or change his smelly nappy. Sofie's really naughty now. She said something really really bad to Mum the last time. I can't say the word. I'm not even going to say what letter it starts with. Sometimes I get cross 'cos Mum calls me all the time to run upstairs and look for something for Davey or the twins to wear as *he's* always being sick because of tolerance or they have an accident and sometimes I get cross too especially if I'm trying to read my book or me and Freda are playing. Do you remember that time Tony flung you out the window when he and Mum had a row and he told her it's time she growed up? OMG Mum went ballistic! She said she's had you since she was little and *howdare he howdarehe!* come into her life and throw her stuff and her kids' stuff around! She said she'll swing for him or anyone who harms her kids. Well that's why I'm always looking out for you, though half the time I can't remember where I left you. I blame the twins; I know they come in my room when I'm at school. I should get you a sword or a laser gun. We'll have to do something about your hair. Mum told me that old story what happened and first she was laughing and then she was crying and I had to go and sit on her lap and give her a cuddle and she said her dad had given you to her and her sisters got so jealous they painted all your lovely hair with nail polish and their mum had to cut it out. So that's why you're so spiky; Mum says you look like a punk. I don't know what a punk is. Anyway, she said her dad never believed her but what do you expect when her sisters' mum wasn't her mum and what sort of mum walks out and leaves her kids anyway? She'll die for us, she swears. She'll kill for us too.

So me and Mum are like this, see? OK, OK just pretend you can cross your fingers. Come, I'll read you some of my new Jacqueline Wilson. Sofie got it for me. I like the smell of new books. Mum accused her of nicking it from Smiths when she was out with her friend Aster who lives in care but Sofie said she never, how she bought it with her babysitting money, but Mum didn't believe her and they had another fight and Sofie left. Again.

I do miss Sofie. I miss cuddling up to her in bed. I miss her coming with me to Dad's too because she won't stand no nonsense from that Melissa. But I miss her specially 'cos every time when there's fighting she covered my ears or she would put on CBeebies louder. The times with the twins' dad was the worst. I won't say his name. I can't say his name as bad magic happens sometimes when you say names. So I just call him *Him*. Mum calls him *It*. Mum's got a scar on the back of her neck from that time. And me too, look, on my arm. I don't think it'll ever fade. He did it with the iron though he said he didn't mean to, was an accident. I don't think the twins can remember him. They just speak to each other in gobbledegook. Mum says she's waiting to see so many specialists she bet she's keeping them in holidays and tax havens.

When we have the party it's going to be fan-*tas*-tic. Mum has been buying stuff from Wilkinson's and Asda's in the sales for ages. We've got tea-lights and candles and glow-in-the-dark stickers. We've got party bags and balloons and whistles and sweets and bubbly glasses and fairy lights and streamers and masks. Everybody's dressing up like someone from a fairytale. Mum said nobody's allowed to come if they don't dress up. She wanted to get a wizard but couldn't afford him so Alex next door is going to do some tricks. I asked her why a wizard not a witch and she said they weren't the same. She wanted to get a pony too but we wouldn't have been able to get him down the stairs.

Gotto go. Mum's calling me.

***

There you are! How the *heck* did you get in there? I've been searching and searching all over everywhere. But then there was school and the dentist and shopping and Tony came back again on Saturday and he and Mum was laughing and drinking wine and I had Davey in bed with me and Freda and we was eating popcorn and of course they all wrecked my room. Then next day, Tony shouted at me and Freda to tidy our rooms and how popcorn was everywhere and he made me even take stuff out from underneath the bed and that's how I found you. Well you can't wear that dress now. It's a flippin disgrace. We can't have the world looking down on us.

★★★

They started arguing again. It's getting like with Freda's dad. But this time it's Tony. It started with the stuff Mum ordered online. They was magic wands that lit up, well neat they was and Mum said how cool it would look when the party got dark ... did I tell you the party is going to last till it got dark? That is going to be amazing! If me and you get some glow-in-the-dark stickers we can stick it on our skin and hide and scare everyone when we jump out. Tony's going to put the fairy lights round the tree in the back garden. Well anyway, the delivery van came and Tony answered the door and who should be standing at the door at the very same time but the man from the Provy?! We never answer the door to the man from the Provy, everyone knows that!

'There he was holding 'is hand out', Mum said, when Clare come round. 'Stood there on my doorstep facing up to Tony how three weeks is owed. Three weeks is owed! Bleeding liar! Am I s'possed to feed my kids or line their pockets? Effing people don't know what it's like to be poor!'

'What did Tony say?' Clare said. (They was in the kitchen drinking tea.)

'Nothing to do with him! He told him. Told him he didn't live here and how the lady of the house wasn't in.

'But you're signing for the parcel, the Provy man said.

Yes I'm signing for the parcel, Mate, Tony said. *That don't mean I live 'ere do it?'*

And then them two started having more and more arguing and the delivery man scarpered and got back in his van and Tony told the Provy man to shift it and the Provy man shouted how they would be getting a letter soon and someone else would be round and then Tony come in and started shouting at Mum.

'This stupid party of yours is getting outahand,' he says. 'How comes you got the money to buy stuff online and what is this crap anyway?'

And then, *'And then!'* Mum said to Clare, 'do you know what that bastard did?'

'What?' said Clare.

They come in the front room then with their tea, and: *Move your stuff off the table, you,* Mum says to me, (only it wasn't my stuff, it was Freda's) and she put the tea down and got her cigarettes out and said, 'He ripped open my mail, *my mail!* Bastard opens my mail, took my stuff out, stuff I got for the kids and snapped them into bits!'

'No!' Clare says, *'He never!'*

'Yes!' says Mum. 'And that was it! That was bloody it! I told him to leg it, if he weren't going to show me and the kids consideration there's no room in our lives for him. My kids have already been messed about, it ain't happening no more. Twelve pounds ninety nine them wands cost me! And if you know what's good fer you you'd better not come back I told him!'

Well. So off Tony goes and Mum borrows a tenner from Clare and orders us a Dominos pizza and we all curl up on the sofa and watch *Incredibles*.

★★★

Now you have to be quiet, all of you. Now, Freda! Boys shush or I won't read you a story! Come here, Davey, sit down next to Barbie.

Once upon a time there was a girl called Snow White. She was the apple of her father's eye...

Freda, it means she was the favourite. Yeah, I know it's not fair...

Shush, Freda, or I won't read! *Sadly he lost his beautiful wife, Snow White's mother...*

It is not boring! I'm getting to the dwarf bit, just wait willya!

SHUT UP, Freda! Stop interrupting!

...the new Queen was extremely beautiful and thrived on people telling her so...

No, I don't know what *thrived* means. It doesn't matter.

I don't know! Just shut up and listen!

Oh for Chrissake! Boys! Stop getting all my stuff out. Stop it you two!

'Scarlett! SCARLETT! Come downstairs, I need you to get some electric for me!'

'I can't, Mum!'

'Yes you can! Just give them a tenner and the key.'

'What if they ask me something? Plus I'm reading the kids a story!'

'They won't ask you nothing and you can read it when you come back!'

'Take Davey', she says, strapping him in. 'And that poor thing,' she adds.

Don't know why we always have to live on a blinking hill. Last two houses we lived was both on hills. You can't ride your bike up them, you can't push the pushchair up them, you can't carry all the shopping all the way from the bus stop without getting tired and the twins whinging. Don't care if Mum says princesses all live in castles on hills. She doesn't have to push Davey all the time. And I don't know why Freda can't look after him more, she is six. When I was six I was doing loads of stuff. Maybe I should have brought my Jacqueline Wilson book and we could have took it to the park. Least I can read in peace there whilst Davey runs round. Oh no, there's that nosey Mrs P...

...

Mum'll be so proud of us, Barbie! We was well polite! I was smiling all the time she was saying 'Hello Scarlett, how are you dear? Taking Davey for a walk? That doll of yours looks a little worse for wear, dear. How's your Mummy? Are you all okay? I heard a lot of shouting the other night ... was it the TV? You do have it on all day, sometimes it is very loud...!'

Is she still looking? You wait till I tell Mum!

...

The twins' costumes came today. They're dwarfs. With them, Georgie, Tony and the dads that makes seven. Imagine that. If we didn't have enough dads we'd have had to borrow some to make seven. Seven is a lucky number. That's why there's seven of us, see. The dads are supposed to get their own costumes though. Mum says she's not paying for them. She's already paid for the bouncy castle out of the family allowance. We're all eating mean this week. Just beans and pasta and stuff. We're not to touch the bottom shelf in the freezer, though it's really hard not to! I have a peep when I go for Davey's milk. There are mini sausages and cheesecake and chicken dippers in there already. And some of them spicy things that Tony and Mum like. I don't know about Clare.

We all fell about laughing when the twins tried on their costumes ... we've already got a Grumpy that's Nathan, and a Happy, that's Joshua, so Mum said she don't need to put no make-up on them. But the legs were too big and Joshee kept falling over and Nate put his head through the sleeve and the same time Davey came crawling through the living room with his nappy off and peed all over Joshee's feet.

★★★

I'm going to crawl in here with you Barbie. No one'll know where we are. Get snuggy, have some cover. Let's be really, really quiet. Everybody's really upset. Mum's mega mega crazy mad. The kind of mad that lasts for ages. It started when me and Freda got called out our class at school today and had to sit in the Staff Room. We didn't know why, Miss just said, 'Sit down, girls, somebody wants to talk to you.'

And then, these two people came in, a man and a lady, and said, 'Don't worry, we just want to see if you're all right, if you're happy at school and is everything OK at home?'

Me and Freda just looked at each other. Freda gets really shy sometimes but though she's younger than me she's growed up because she has to do all the talking but then she just said she liked Barbies and skipping and playtime and the man asked her why we didn't come to school last Wednesday and Freda said she didn't know and then she said, 'Oh, was that when we woke up late because Davey was sick in the night and woke us all up and we were tired and why, are we in trouble?'

And the lady said, 'Don't worry, Freda, no one's in trouble but everyone's got to go to school you see and we don't want Mummy to get into trouble.' And then she said, 'Have you been seeing your dad lately?'

And me and Freda looked at each other and I could see her lip was trembling like just before she cries and we didn't know whose dad she meant and I sneaked my hand so it was touching hers and my heart was banging away *bang bang bang bang* inside me and I didn't know what to think, what did she mean about Mummy getting into trouble, why should she get into trouble? I know sometimes we can't go to school if Mummy has a bad night like when she and Tony fight or if she's tired from wine or Davey wakes up and I have to bring him in my bed and then he wants a bottle and then Freda wakes up and starts kicking me and sometimes the twins wake up too and start getting all their toys out even though it's still dark and sometimes the electric goes and we can't wash our school clothes and sometimes we can't find our shoes. And why were they looking at me? They know I can't tell them. And why are they asking me about my dad, he's got his tag off now and can go where he likes. Or do they know; do they know about the other thing, the thing we're never ever supposed to talk about?

And when we go home and tell Mum she goes crazy. We got cut off the phone so she only had her mobile and she put on her school voice like *Yes this is Mrs Rollins here and I understand that my children were taken out of their classes today without my permission and you know that Scarlett ...* and then she was put on hold then her minutes went and she smashed the phone down on the floor and started talking in her normal voice saying how dare they add to my little girls' anxieties and some effing person must have reported her, some effing sadoh person with no life and if anyone thinks they can take her kids off her they don't know what she's capable of, the fockers. And then she picked up her shoe and started banging the wall between us and Mrs P. Joshee started crying then and Mum picked him up and was walking up and down trying to shush him and he was kicking her and we could see she was crying too then she gave him to me and lit up the half of the cigarette she was saving.

The thing is about Mum she doesn't forget. You think she forgets and later we're turning the music up high, Ed Sheeran and Rizzlekicks – and we're all having a dance and we're killing ourselves laughing as Mum shows us how she used to dance when she went clubbing, and even the twins are wiggling their hips and Mum dives in the clean clothes pile and digs a pair of her knickers out and puts it over her head and her eyes are like Spiderman's and we're laughing so much Freda starts to cough and cough and Mum sits her down on the sofa because of her asthma and says OK let's all calm down now and she sends Georgie out to get some KFC to cheer us up but he's gone ages we thought he just went round his friends instead with the money so we raid the bottom freezer and treat ourselves to the chicken dippers we was saving for the party with curly chips and popcorn. But Mum can't forget so she goes next door and bangs on the door *bang bang bang* and shouts out *I know you're in there you vicious old cow!* But Mrs P won't open it and Tony follows Mum and grabs her hand and say let's watch a dvd, come on. And he brings her back inside and calms her down, and gives her one of his special cans and says, *you don't even know it was her, could be anybody.* And even though I still can't speak to him at least he helps Mum 'cos sometimes we don't know what to do.

And then we sat down to watch a movie *as a family*, only we can't get Box Office so we dig out *Night at the Museum* 1 and 2 and snuggle down on the sofa with our duvets, Mum too, and then Georgie comes in with the KFC only we don't want it 'cos we're full up and Tony shouts at Georgie and Georgie slams the door and stamps up to his room. Mum rewinds the bit of dvd we missed where the dinosaur is chasing him down the corridor and we settle back down again. We all fell asleep then on the sofa and the floor but it didn't matter as it was Friday and when we woke up it was Saturday and someone was banging on the door *Bang Bang Bang Bang* and Tony tripped over the boxes of KFC they'd forgot to put in the fridge and the cats had ate it and throwed up and there was bones and sick all up the stairs and when Tony opened the door who do you think was standing there but coppers!

'We have a complaint,' they sez, and oh it's funny now, how Tony tells it. 'We have had a complaint,' they sez, 'that someone was banging on the wall of Number 4 and playing music loud all night. We have a very upset elderly lady next door and if it were not for the fact that we had several emergencies last night – being Friday – my colleague and I would have got here much sooner. Can we come in?'

But it wasn't funny then, Mum came to the door rubbing

her eyes, holding Davey, and stares at the coppers like she was dreaming. Then she looks at one of the coppers and sez, 'Didn't I use to go to school with you?' Then she puts on her telephone voice and accuses next door of harassing her, of being intolerant of children, of being unsympathetic to the fact that she was singlehandedly raising her children, some of which has special needs, with no help from anyone, and invites the coppers in for a cup of tea.

I love my mum. She's like a rollercoaster she is. She's making the coppers tea as nice as anything and saying 'please excuse the state of the place, me and Tony and the kids had a sleep-over last night, and fancy you becoming a copper, you was a well daredevil at school', and the coppers stretch their legs out and drink their tea and say, 'well take it easy with the old lady, my mum's like that, take her some flowers or something', and that was that.

Oh, I wish you could tell me what my mum was like when she was little! She don't like to talk about it. You know, I'm not being mean but the bestest time I've had with her was before Tony and Davey and Freda's dad and even before Freda and especially before the twins and *him*. I do love them to bits I do but ... I loved it when it was just Sofie, Georgie and me. That's when we lived in that little flat in East ... something. I look at them photos sometimes, there's that one with my dad standing there by his motorbike with me and Georgie on the seat. I asked Mum why didn't she wait for Dad to come back and she just screws up her face and says ask *him*. I bet you could tell me stuff. Sometimes I pretend I'm sick so I don't have to go to school and then it's just me, Mum and Davey on the sofa watching Mum's favourite film *Gone with the Wind*, and Mum's crying at the end and saying how she used to look so much like Vivien Leigh and all the guys were after her and that's why she called me Scarlett. Then she would squeeze me so tight and say, 'Scarlett, honey, you mustn't make my mistakes, you just carry on with being good at school, you'll be all right I promise', and I say 'Yes, Mum, but it's really hard.' And she rewinds the last bit of the film when Scarlet stands at the front door and squints her eyes up and says, *Oh I can't think about it now, I'll go crazy if I think about it now! ...I'll think about it tomorrow. Tomorrow is another day!*

Mum stands up then and looks round our front room and pats the wall and straightens our photos and says something about Tara and laughs and walks in the kitchen.

Only one week till the party! I can't wait! My three friends from school are Carrie, Lydia and Sophia (like Sofie) and they are all coming as princesses. They got their dresses from ASDA too but I think Lydia's is lilac. Carrie and Lydia and Sophia was talking about it in the playground. Sometimes I whisper when it's just us four but my teacher was listening and she said it sounds like it going to be a lot of fun. Then she said I must try and get Mummy to listen to me and Freda read our books or we would get behind.

She doesn't understand that Mum hasn't got time to read with us. She's always on the phone trying to sort things out with money and clinics and things and she's been really busy wallpapering her bedroom and our front room all by herself. Weeks and weeks she's sticking samplers on the wall from B & Q. We come home from school and there's stripes and then there's dragonflies and butterflies. There's blobs of cream and lime-green and blue 'cos she can't decide what colour. Plus she's got the twins and Davey to look after and has to walk up and down the hill three times a week to take the twins to nursery. *And* she's got all the washing and the cooking and the shopping and the hoovering. Georgie doesn't help do anything except put the rubbish out and feed the cats. *And*, he's got girls coming round after school all the time now! They stand at the front door and giggle. Before Sofie left, she would read to me and now I read to Freda and try to get her to form her words and write in her Reading Record that *Freda really likes this book and can read two new words.* Only I can't get Freda to sit still, she doesn't listen and just goes off playing with you and her Baby New Born and that's when we fight. She's not allowed to play with you when I'm not here because I can never find you after. And when I can't find you it's like my mouth has swallowed pepper, like that time in Nandos when I bit a jalapeno and I screamed the words out *Mum, my mouth is burning!* And everyone starts looking at me and their faces are spinning round the table and turning into monsters like clowns and all their gums are red like blood and all I can see is *him him him* standing over my mum in the kitchen with that knife saying *I'll slice that beautiful face of yours, you mad bitch.*

Sofie came round the other night. Mum didn't want to let her in because the last time she said she would throw a stone through the window. She came in the back door with her friend Aster who Mum said smells. At first she sat down on the sofa and said hello and when Mum asked her what she was doing with her life she just lifted up her shoulder and then she went and gave Mum a cuddle. Then they started crying and Mum said you can't go on like this Sofie, and Sofie says I know, I know, but have you got £10? Can you let me have £10? Please. And then they started fighting again and I came to find you then, it's dark and warm down here and if I shut the door I can't hear anything.

★★★

Our phone's working again. Dad gave Mum some money so she could pay some bills and even the Provy man got some. Dad said isn't it time that useless tosser Tony got a job and Mum laughed and said *you're a one to talk aintcha.* We all went down town in a black cab and paid Brighthouse and got some more stuff from Asda. The twins did our heads in running round touching stuff and Davey screaming all the time 'cos he wanted to get out the trolley. He was kicking and kicking his legs and trying to climb out. Mum promised to get us some mini doughnuts if we behaved. People was looking at us. People are always looking at us. Sometimes on the bus they say to Mum, how can you manage with all of them? And they look at me and say, she's so beautiful, and so quiet. Well they're all different ain't they, dear. Then we got a black cab again and came home and watched Sky which was on again so we could watch the Disney Channel. We was all settled down then all happy with Mum yakking on the phone to Clare about the party, how she might invite that nice-looking copper who she used to go to school with. She was laughing and saying about going up in the world when the doorbell rings and guess who turned up but one of my aunties who Mum sez think their shit don't stink.

I can't remember the last time I saw my Auntie Marina. Mum says she's just full of herself with her posh job and her car but she's always nice to us. On my last birthday she sent me ten pounds and wrote me in the card to buy myself something nice but Tony borrowed it. I think he did it to try and make me speak to him. She brought us a big tin of Quality Street and Mum sent me in the kitchen to make tea. When I came back they was talking about the party and Auntie Marina was saying, 'don't you think it's a bit of an extravagance, Ella,?' And she looked up at our TV on the wall and at Georgie sunk into the sofa playing with his Nintendo. Hollyoaks was on and she said to Mum, 'Do you still watch that rubbish?' Mum's face was a picture, only her lips was moving even though they was tight shut.

Marina don't know the signs, she can't read Mum like I can. She carried on, 'Don't you guys watch the news? Hey, Georgie, who's the Prime Minister?'

Georgie just raised up his shoulders and looked back down at his game, and Mum stood up and said, 'Right you, Out!' And she lifted her arm and pointed her finger at Auntie Marina. 'There's the door,' she said, 'you're not coming round here putting me down, I've had enough!'

We heard her slam the front door and she came back in rubbing her hands together. 'Well that's one off the list,' she said, 'Who wants a mini doughnut?'

★★★

Today in school I got called out again. Only me, not Freda. I was shaking, standing in the corridor, but Miss Parker said, don't worry, Scarlett, Mummy knows, didn't she tell you? Oh dear, never mind, here this is Mrs Williams ... she's just going to do your sounds with you from now on. And we went in the room near her office where people go when they're not well and there was drawing stuff on the table and some cds and books and I can't remember all the things she said and what she was reading. They know I like stories but all the time I knew what she wanted me to do. She wanted me to cough up the words deep inside but they wouldn't come. I could feel them bouncing round like peas in my tummy. I looked up at her, she had a nice face but it was not Mummy's face, it wasn't Sofie's face or Georgie's face or Freda's face or the twins' or Davey's face or Dad's face or your face. So the words stayed there, wobbling round like bingo balls until she said Okay Scarlett, it's perfectly all right, perhaps next week you can bring in one of your favourite books or a toy maybe? And I nodded then, thinking Oh good, I can bring you in maybe.

***

O I am so so sleepy BB. Haven't we had a well good time! It was like super chocolate sick amazing! You looked like a real princess in your new dress, with your tiara. It didn't matter about your hair, and Sindy's shoes fit you and your toes got clean and the silver nail polish looks so sparkly I can even see you in the dark. I am so so happy that nothing, absolutely nothing went wrong! Isn't that amazing? Everyone who came was nice, there was no fighting. Nathan only cried once when Georgie jumped on him on the bouncy castle. My friends loved it, they said it was the best party ever and they loved their party bags and their masks with their names on. And Davey walked! Davey walked! Mum cried, and she and Tony watched him walk three steps before he fell over and he didn't even cry. And we had loads of ice cream and crisps and Lydia won Statues and Mum took Mrs P some cake and my dad was drinking with Tony and Freda's ginger straw blond dad came with his girlfriend and Mum did a toast to Tara and Tony said who the eff is Tara and Mum and me smiled at each other and even though Sofie wore exactly the same dress and make-up as Mum only with more make-up, it was fine and I'm still so excited I don't know if I can sleep but when I close my eyes I see my mum and her thumbs are up and she's saying *tomorrow is another day.*

★★★

Selective Mutism is a psychological, anxiety-based disorder mostly common amongst children who have suffered some form of deep stress. They may speak normally to close family members and occasionally whisper to close associates but are unable to communicate with anyone else outside the family unit.

MOVING ON

He was lying on a bed of ferns, and ravens were picking his bones clean. He felt no pain, just a silent joy at the glimpses of sky between their trembling wings. Only the earth was angry. It juddered beneath him with the sharpness of elbows, prising itself between his ribs, ejecting him with a force.

The black wings came closer, with a sheen and an unexpected softness, and the slitted blue of the sky bore down above him, cold and angry.

'For Chrissake,' she said, 'will you stop snoring!'

The morning was gloomy, and he stood in his dressing gown and fleece at the door whilst he let the dog out. The birds were at the feeders already, blue tits and the blackbird, a pair of nuthatches. A robin flew down as he watched, poised on the fence, undecided. The song of the river rippled at the edge of his consciousness, across the lane, around the back of the farmhouse. He wondered how it would have been to have been able to buy that instead, been able to watch the heron at will, listen to the full choral of the river's song instead of its chorus. The dog cocked his leg on the untidy patch of grass that was their front garden, in the shadow of his van.

He sensed Sara behind him, knew what she was going to say before she said it. 'Do you have to leave the door open? It's cold enough in this place!'

He drove out towards Henllan, the morning lifting, random patches of blue at the edges of the fields, the crown of hedges. The van coughed up the hill, the countryside dropping below him with a lilt that calmed his heart. He patted the wheel, 'Good girl, you can make it.'

Over the stone bridge, an embrace of trees shouldering the sky; the river below rushing, over stones and rocks. He walked there sometimes, parked the van left of the bridge, held the halter tight against the dog's wild leap, passed the cottage which over the years had decomposed from being white-washed and lived-in, to a desolate ruin with boarded-up windows and wild bamboo enclosing what was once a garden. He appreciated its abandonment. Like so many others, it was once a picturesque dwelling on the side of a quiet country road, infrequently interrupted by tractors, now shaken by the constant onslaught of four by fours, lorries, the 460 bus to Carmarthen. But once through the five-barred gate, you entered a sacred, primeval world, filtered sunbursts of light; tall, canopied trees, pines that pierced the sky, luxuriant ferns fringing the rough track scored by pools and fissures. The dog ran free off his lead. The river roared its passage, tumbling past to launch itself over the waterfall. He cautioned himself against being fanciful, the woodland was well maintained; only last year an overcrowded section had been logged, stockpiled into creating new homes for the wildlife he imagined, beetles and woodlice, an amorphous world of fungi... A shame those concerned weren't quick enough to remove the fallen trees which for two years now had blocked the path, forcing dog lovers and welly-booted children to scramble over and under, slide on hands and knees where the track disappeared into the riverbank. But, he loved it, how he loved it! That stillness only broken by the river's rumble, and the mad scramble and excited barking of his dog. He liked nothing better than to pause where the river was still, and train his binoculars where he imagined kingfishers to be. He had begun to love this country.

It was a far cry from Pinner, suburbia multiplying like a cancer, vehicles nose to tail, his hands heavy on the steering wheel. He used to attempt to calculate how many hours he had spent waiting at traffic lights, or cruising behind buses.

All so different now. He breathed in the country air as he drove through Henllan. His keen eyes could spot the bags at the roadside from two hundred yards. If he was lucky there would be two or three crowded together, their contents defining themselves by their shapes: angular and sharp: pictures, books, frames, toys; rounded, soft: abandoned Care Bears, cushions, old bedding, sometimes a quilt which Mairead would toss into the recycling pile, her thin lips twisting her normally sanguine face. There might be a box of mismatched crockery, tied up with string, the bottom sagging as he lifted it. And videos; the inevitable cast-off videos. He'd been told to leave them now, there were signs up in the shop: No more videos. Try telling that to the old dears who knew him well now, stood in their porches and waved. Some even phoned him, *clearing out*, they said, *clearing out*. It was kinder to add the unwanted items to Mairead's mountainous recycling pile. He sometimes wondered how the public would feel if they knew how many of their charitable off-loadings went for scrap.

There was a time when charity shops were cheap, Sara constantly said, now it's cheaper to go to Primark. Oh, I forgot, she would add, there's not even a Primark here is there.

His wife was bitter. He understood her bitterness. To use that well-worn phrase, they didn't sign up for this. It would be different if he was old enough for a pension, but he wasn't. Never in a thousand years would he have imagined himself doing the job he did now. There wasn't much call for cargo officers here. He tried not to let thoughts of the past five years cloud his day. They fogged his mind often enough, beat him with sticks of his own failure, a list of wrong decisions which had trapped them here, money gone, property market slumped. Over and over again, they talked, him and Sara, how they could have done it better, if they'd got different builders, if they hadn't done the renovation, if they hadn't come here at all. He thought of her sat in that extension now, drinking coffee, the cigarettes she'd returned to smoking slowly burning down her thin fingers. A dream gone wrong, she summed it up. She was being kind. He knew she felt he had failed her. Her dream of living in the country should have remained a dream, she was a city girl used to coffee bars and theatres. A city girl who didn't drive. Strange how the things you rail against are the very things you miss.

His own experience was different of course, made more complicated by the fact that he felt guilty about his own contentment. He was back to being a boy. He was back to being a boy back in Sussex who left home each day with fishing rod and box to collect birds' eggs, not returning home until teatime. He was back to being a boy who knew the name of every bird and recognised each individual call. He especially liked it in these villages, accessed by narrow roads, him and his van climbing the hills like Postman Pat. Even as he drove he spotted red kites, kestrels, herons. Even as he walked up and down the drives where charity bags sat propped up by gateposts or beckoned from front porches, he did so with a spring in his step. Infrequently small conversations added a different rhythm to his day, Mrs Davies from number 9 waiting to see it was him picking her bag up and not those other louts driving round nicking things to flog at a boot fair. Mr Evans from Pencader, one step forward on the burden of grief, finally placing his deceased wife's clothes into extra bags. *She'd have wanted me to give them to you. Was her heart, you see. They were good to her, those nurses.*

Mairead looked down at him from the top of the stairs. 'How's your catch today, Mr Fisher?'

'Hauling them in,' he retorted.

'Well we've had a weather report. You missed one.'

He sighed. Annoying when that happened. Maybe his eye wasn't as keen as he thought it was.

'And', she went on, enjoying herself, 'you netted one you shouldn't have done.'

'What? Where?'

'By the Murco Garage. Says she left her books out for the library and you nicked 'em.'

'Christ.'

He'd wondered about that one. Stood on the wall in a Tesco's Bag For Life, the charity bags below. But you could never tell.

He removed his woolly hat, and wiped the sweat from his brow. His back ached. Filled with the pleasures of being in the outdoors he didn't realise how much it took out of him until he stopped. There were another fifty or so bags to be unloaded. Somewhere amongst them was a Tesco's bag.

'Cathy called me today,' Sara said over dinner. They were sitting in the extension, Eastenders on. The telly was on all day and night.

'Said Rob was away next week in Edinburgh for work and did I want to come and stay.'

'Oh, yes? Had enough of her has he?' The comment jumped out before he could stop it.

She paused mid-fork. 'You b...! That was totally uncalled-for!'

The apology stuck in his throat. He didn't like Cathy or Rob, never had, their marital affairs were always full of drama. That was one of the reasons he had been glad to leave Pinner, all those false dinner parties and fake laughter.

'How dare you!' Sara pushed her plate away forcefully on the coffee table. Her fork fell to the floor but she ignored it.

'You know, you are growing into a selfish son of a b...! Have you any idea what it's like for me, stuck here by myself all day? This wasn't supposed to be a forever, Jack! I have had enough!'

'Ok Ok, Sara, I shouldn't have said that about Cathy, but what exactly do you want me to do? We can't sell the house, at least not till the market improves, and we need the money, so I've got to do this job. Do you think I am working for fun?'

The words almost stuck in his throat then, as part of him knew he wasn't telling the truth.

'Look, Sara, that part of our life is over, why can't you just adapt?'

'What, leave my whole life behind? I had a life, Jack. I can't just go out and make another! Not like you!'

She stormed into the kitchen and he heard her refill her wine glass.

She wagged her finger at him on her return.

'You know the worst thing about all this? It's you! It's you and that bloody ... thing ... out there! That white van! A white van! At least you could have bought a blue one, or a red one, or one that looked ... not like a van!' She took a glug of wine and carried on. 'You don't even care what you look like! What's with the woolly hats and fleeces? My God!

Even if I did go out and make these supposedly 'new friends' what does that tell them about me? I can't even get anywhere under my own steam! I am so ashamed. I don't know who I am anymore.'

She sank into the sofa and began to cry. The sofa curved itself around her body, used to being sat on. It had been new when they first came here, as perky and resilient as they were.

'I ... am ... not ... a pathetic person,' she muttered in-between sobs.

Jack ran his hand through his hair. His half-eaten dinner sat on his plate, congealing.

He brought her a cup of tea next morning before he left. It was still dark, but she was already awake and on Facebook. She barely acknowledged him.

'I have to leave a bit earlier this morning,' he said, 'missed a few yesterday.'

She ignored him.

'Look, why don't you book a train ticket today, go and spend a few days with Cathy.'

'Is there enough money in the account?'

'Should be, I haven't paid the phone bill yet.'

He rung the bell, Tesco's bag in hand. He could hear dogs yapping and a voice shouting to keep it down. When the door opened, he was surprised to find himself looking down at a woman in a wheelchair.

'Hello, I brought your library books back, I'm really sorry, they were with the charity bags...'

'Well, not exactly,' she snapped, 'they were actually on the wall.'

'I can but apologise...'

Suddenly a small terrier bounced through the hallway and squeezed itself between the wheels. Through a tuft of black and white spiky hair, two small black eyes glared at him. A low growl rumbled from the back of its throat.

'Shut up, Strike!'

He could hear more barking coming from the dark recesses of the hallway.

'You sound like you've got a houseful.'

'There's only three of them. Keep me company. Husband died and bloody left me to cope.'

He shifted on the doorstep, not sure what to say.

'Not from round here, are you? Well you want to make sure you can settle before you dig yourself in, like me.'

He walked down the driveway, feeling unsettled.

The week Sara was away began well for him. He'd seen her off at the station. The sun was shining. She was smiling, dressed in her best jeans and Next jacket. She'd climbed down from the van with a sigh of relief. Waved him off jauntily from the door of the train. He drove into B and Q car park and bought himself a sausage roll and a coffee. Nothing like a bit of junk food to cheer you up. He was picking up round Carmarthen that day, not his favourite place. It was the houses. It was the busy road. It was the traffic. His tolerance level for busyness was getting lower and lower. Pinner seemed a world away. He was happiest out in the countryside, with the fields and the singing birds and the staggered clusters of cottages. He no longer wanted pavements with dog poo and short-tempered drivers and other white vans like his, cruising, pretending they were picking up for children in Romania.

He put fish pies in the microwave and listened to the radio. He took the dog down to Henllan and watched the birds. He posted delivery bags out around Cilgerran and exchanged friendly greetings with elderly men and women over fences. His neighbours passed the time of day, mentioned they had a few things to clear out. Like him and Sara, not many of them were local, there was the couple from Yorkshire, another from Reading, and a woman called Laura from Banbury. The one original Welsh neighbour invited him round for tea and showed him photos of the mill in its heyday. She shook her head sadly as she showed him where the village shop used to be, and the paddock, all bought off now, bungalows going up in their place. Oh, that was all another time, she said, it's all changing so fast now, I don't recognise it.

By Thursday he was missing Sara. Missed her moodiness even. He sat and watched Eastenders for company.

She postponed her return, changed her ticket. Cathy needs me, she said on the phone, that bastard's seeing someone from his office.

When she returned, he was happy to see her. He stood on the platform and watched her step down from the train. She looked like she used to, smart and pretty. She was chatty, filling him in about old friends, the new play she'd seen. They made love, something they hadn't done for ages.

'Why don't you come out with me today?' He brought her a cuppa, felt a stirring of desire as she lay, her hair messy on the pillow. She raised her eyebrows, and looked out the window. The sun was shining.

Within a couple of weeks, she left again. This time to stay with her sisters. By October she had fallen into a pattern, three weeks with him, one week away. Each time she returned, a little less of her came back; a new haircut, her large suitcase. Each time she left he slipped into a rhythm of not missing her, of missing her. Cooked concoctions she laughed at over the telephone. He tried to relay the stories he was coming into contact with on a daily basis, stories filtered through the bags he collected for the charity, people waiting on their doorstep to hand him something of particular relevance, a nephew going to university, a divorce, a partner dying, their old shoes and suits carefully folded in cardboard and plastic. Part of him believed he was being useful, providing a service.

And then that November morning. She came out with him in the van, her face cold and pinched. He was his cheery best, pointing out the kestrel above them past Cenarth, the waterfall heavy with rain, the tale of the salmon they'd found flipped on the car park. Her replies were non-committal, her face stared straight ahead. He drove through Cardigan town centre, struggled up the hill. He felt her eyes on him as he pulled to a stop, leapt out and began to gather the bags from the roadside. The sun was coming out. He wandered up and down the pavements, coming back with bags of varying shapes, cardboard boxes; piled them into the back, slammed the door shut.

He was whistling as he got back in the driving seat.

'You love it, don't you?'

'What?' He was cruising down the next street, eyes searching.

'This job, being here, everything.'

There was a crowd outside one of the houses, people with their arms round each other.

'I can tell.'

He pulled to a stop, watching the crowd.

'It's just not the same for me, Jack.'

He climbed out of the van. There were bags on the pavement. In the front garden a young girl sat, crying. One of the women turned to him as he approached.

'What's all that about?' Sara asked as he climbed back into his seat. He sat still, perfectly still.

'Jack...?'

'Christ,' he said, shaking his head.

He turned to her.

'A young boy's been killed.'

'What?!'

'Run over, this morning, on the main road.'

'Oh my God...! Is that, are they...?'

He nodded, slowly, thinking of the bags he'd just been handed, full of belongings sorted out just yesterday apparently – boxes of games, a gameboy ... moving up to big school, the woman had said. He sat frozen behind the wheel. A boy. All his life ahead of him. Christ. He wondered if the boy's mother would regret it, giving his things away. Imagined Mairead receiving the phone call, a week, a month down the line...

'Jack...' Sara was nudging him. His hands moved automatically, turned the key.

The boy's death weighed on them both. Something shifted. He thought he was used to the changing pattern of life he dealt with daily, all those personal belongings moved on, the books, the shoes, the Action Man figures. But he couldn't get it out of his head that hour he'd been driving around whistling, collecting bags, the boy had been walking towards his death. That TV programme came to mind, Death in Paradise. He told himself not to be so crass.

He had hoped that, somehow, the experience would have brought him and Sara closer, that she would appreciate what he did a bit more. If anything, she grew even more morose. The weather turned, the river in their lane burst its banks and rushed with maleficent abandon, settling on their garden, lingering on the foundations of the extension. She had turned to him and said, 'Don't you see, this is not my life! I am being sucked in, I'm drowning!'

There's something to be said for seeing a country at its worst. That winter was the winter of floods. He drove through sheets of rain returning from the station, worried about the engine. A flock of Canada geese trumpeted overhead. Glimpses of the ghostly track of the abandoned railway running past Newcastle Emlyn filtered through the trees. He wondered how many lives its closure had changed, whether it would have made any difference to theirs. The fields at Cilgerran were a sea of water, the level rising almost to the lip of the old arched bridge. When the sun shone, it lit on the water, gracing it with a mirrored incandescence that tantalised the senses into thinking it beautiful.

Panic had risen within him for a moment after she boarded, He couldn't see her – her body was swallowed up by the carriage, subsumed and anonymous in a group of strangers. He remembered thinking, he could understand why early Native Americans feared the railroad, the dragon. Then he saw her settled in a window seat. She looked at him and raised her hand briefly, her face partly erased by the glass. The train began its glide out of the station, and he remained on the platform, as he always did, watching it grow smaller and smaller down the track until it ceased to exist.

EPILOGUE
ON INHABITING A COUNTRY OF WORDS

When my grandmother came to visit she walked. That rolling country woman walk brimmed by a Panama hat that situated us in the tropics. I would spot her turning the corner of Main St, where the Church of the Ascension rose up behind her like a sailing ship, belfried tower like Columbus' galleon. Her large body rolled down St John Street like a dug-out butting the waves (before they paved the road the potholes as large as Victoria lilies) and soon she would land at our gate, stepping on the bridge under which the open gutter tumbled with rainwater, spit, fish heads, bandages, and Juicee bottle tops. Sometimes we would drop our jacks, or the ball would roll, and we would dare one another to reach down our hand and feel amongst the nastiness, daring ringworm and jiggers to ketch we.

When my grandmother visited it was like Christmas. Sweets tumbled out of her bosom like a never-ending string of fairy lights. Those who got caught to her bosom, breathed in Johnsons baby powder and sweat. Her short -sleeved frock would have a big wet underarm patch that bled like a dark rose. I would recognise the smell of buses and tobacco. Buses rolled through our little town and its criss-cross roads by the river, heading for the open Corentyne road with its villages of prayer flags and rice and sugarcane fields, where Indian people called 'coolies' bent double in the hot sun, hacking and setting fire. The tobacco came from the thin cigarettes she rolled between her hardened fingers when time came to rest in the rocking chair by the window, Mummy's chair when *Dr Paul* came on the radio, Daddy's chair when he came home. When I started to get interested in pop music, I would sit there by that radio too, turning the dials by the *Phillips* monogram, tuning in to Herman's Hermits and the Dave Clark Five coming from Radio Parimaribo. (It didn't matter I didn't understand Dutch.)

Before the time I was four I could scrawl my name with chalk on slate at Bowlings Nursery School, the Water St end of our road. By seven I could read good, the Sisters at my next school lashed our knuckles with rulers, and letters and words would jump between my mind and my eyes like those dancing lights you get when you close your eyes and you want sleep to come but it wouldn't. The words lived out there in the spaces between books and sunshine, flinging themselves on the stones, between hard rain that pelted the yard, between church bells ringing, and between the fuzz of Father Andrew gliding along the altar on Sundays, words dropping out of his mouth like pebbles, chipping the edges of the pew as they fell. We were frightened bad, his words held us fast to our seats like glue, as anything un-toward was blasphemy; any wandering thoughts on the deliciousness of altar boys or niggling doubt that God was listening to each and every thought, would only have to come out in the confessional next Saturday, bow down on your knees back there in the latticework cage. But sweet sweet too was the chanting, *Kyrie Eleison*, *Christie Eleison*, over and over again.

I was in admiration of the word *Grandmother*. I was in admiration of the fact that two words that had separate meanings could mean something different when put together. Sometimes there was something called a hyphen that linked them, like a bridge. In some books they were joined up and I thought they looked more powerful then. I also liked the separate meanings of 'grand' and 'mother'. I liked the thought of greatness, and grandeur; that's why I thought of ships, because big ships would sometimes hang on the ocean above our town, like a spaceship or a gleaming star.

Our own mother was the centre of our universe, a universe interrupted by the coursing through of our father who sailed in off the river with sailors at his heels, bottles of rum and his guitar. I preferred those homecomings to the ones that tightened us around him like a belt and all the freedoms we had to run wild in the neighbourhood temporarily fastened and chastised us to speak when we're spoken to and mind our Ps and Qs.

Those Ps and Qs would join the letters that swum around the movement of my getting-tall body as it moved through the rooms of our house and down through the yard into the street with our homemade carts, our cats dressed up in dolly clothes. Sometimes it seemed they had a life of their own, both P and Q seemed like boys, tall skinny boys with sour mouths who would run and tell tales as soon as they had anything to tell and who had the freedom to climb mango and coconut trees.

I couldn't talk about these invaders of course; Mummy would think I was mad, what stupidness are you talking about, girl? she would say. But I couldn't think of a better word. There was a calypsonian called Lord Invader and he was always upsetting people with his words. Another thing what happen was that my fingers, my own fingers, drew words in the air. They mimicked the joining up of letters into words and scripted the air in the style of joined-up writing. They did them behind my back as they knew they couldn't allow themselves to be seen. Not that that didn't cause trouble. What are you hiding behind your back, child? Lemme see. Bare palms glistening in the morning sun, no sign of stolen baby teething powder, a found ten cent piece or nugget of Demerara sugar. I had to find clever ways to not draw attention to my fingers who at all times of the day seemed to want to draw joined-up letters to make the word *luscious*, or *precious*, making sure you got the order right, the *o* before the *u*. So I bade them, be still. Be Still fingers! Just *imagine* you are drawing your beautiful letters out into the air where they dry and temporarily inhabit the space between earth and sky like the aeroplanes that cross us overhead, on their way to Brazil. However. However ... sometimes these ... invaders, these lovely words, these ... ps and qs and lyrical looping of ls and ks, this grouping of *grand* and *mother* that mirrored the essence of my grand-mother, the trembly sensation of burying our heads into her bosom and being anointed, or rustling in the front pockets of her seersucker frock for smarties and fowlcock sweeties, following her glorious and momentous arrival, her Johnson baby powder smell, her unfolding of the cloth over the basket of eggs, her chuckly laughter, her sudden fart when she bent over to rub her feet – had an odd jumbling up in my mind after I had read, all by myself, a book Mummy buy from a travelling American salesman, *The Complete Children's Fairy Tales Complete with Illustrations.*

Complete with Illustrations knocked hells bells out of ps and qs. Of *grand* and *mother*. Because there, on the opposite page of the title 'Red Riding Hood', and 'Once Upon a Time', was a picture of the wolf, who, having eaten RRH's grandmother, was sat back against the cushions on her bed, dressed in her cap and cloak, bedclothes pulled high up against his chest. When reading the words, 'O grandmother, what big eyes you have', and 'O grandmother, what fierce teeth you have', I could not help but think of my own grandmother, my luscious, lovely grandmother, and on first reading of this nasty tale, flung the book across the living room where it lay agape on the Morris chair, the wolf's eyes fixed on the ceiling.

Chastisement fell immediately upon me from my mother, who, although a fair and beautiful mother who smelt of Avon perfume and wore extremely exquisite dresses copied from Movie magazines, and who marched us to church each and every Sunday and was not as fast a hand with the wild cane as my father, nevertheless could turn into a wild cat when aroused. At the same time as she is slapping my arms and legs with the soles of her plastic slippers, the words that are falling out of her mouth are soldiers ready for war, *you know how much! Money don't grow on tree. Betterment, nice things. Endup, Orealla. Slap slap slap!*

Those words were not beautiful, although the way they fell through the air was in perfect synchronisation with her slaps. *Money.* Slap. *Destroy.* Slap. *Orealla.* Slap. *Your Captain father.*

The lesson was that if I didn't appreciate knowledgeable and educational things bought at great expense, to help me, us, (my sisters were of course included in this) make my way onwards and upwards through the world, I would end up as uneducated and as far from civilization as were people who live in Orealla.

All I knew about Orealla was that it existed at the very distant end of the Corentyne road, past 63 Beach, mud houses, sugar and rice plantations, near Surinam; it was where civilization ran into jungle. However, I did think the word sounded especially beautiful, with the most musical and rhythmic intonation and I longed to keep that word on my lips, and play with its syllables like a slow-sucked lollipop – *O Realla. O Re alla.* But of course I didn't think exactly that, at that time, as I hadn't learnt words like 'intonation', yet. Just like I didn't know the truth and reality of Orealla, just the beauty of its name. *What nonsense are you talking, girl? Double Dutch?*

There was another reason why my grandmother occupied a continuous and admirable space in my imaginings. She cussed. O nothing like you would hear now. O Lordy no. But cussing then, even to take the Lord's name in vain, was blasphemy, a venial sin. You couldn't say 'Jesus Lord' unless you were ready for the sting of the cane or carbolic on your tongue. That she was a holy woman who kept her rosary with her at all times and whose altar at home was decorated with crucifixes, bible and candles, was quite at odds with cussing. 'Blasted', 'jackass', 'batty', and once, 'O rass!' invoked paroxysms of stifled giggling from my sisters and me.

When I was eleven years old I won a scholarship to a posh girls' school in the city. That school and that city were as far away from Orealla and New Amsterdam as the moon and the stars. Several things had happened between my learning to read and reaching this improbable and terrifying goal. Words and I had had as tumultuous a journey as the travelling my grandmother did, not least that of the colour of her skin, and the way our country was striving ever upwards for glory and the right to tell its own story. Cussing and learning what men and women do to each other in bedrooms and backrooms, cane shacks and bars, came in drifts of forbidden and tentacled words, in whispers and mouths washed out with soap. The girlfriend who told me the first unbelievable lie, as we dug earth and cooked leaves in our yard, who used the words 'lolee' and 'pussy', using her fingers to make circles through which one finger moved in and out, would be beaten with a belt because of me as her own mother rained down words of hellfire and damnation. The information had been torn from my own petrified lips, words and images scarred permanently on my sponge-like soul.

That year of the scholarship, almost one hundred miles away to the capital Georgetown, a journey over water and rail through thick-leafed banana plantations, to a city of tall buildings and intricate wooden balconies, would reap enormous repercussions. My parents' pride at the scholarship, and my father's promotion to Commodore, are all mixed up with my grandmother moving up the Kwakwani River. There, on a riverbank, rainforest behind her, she set up shop for Amerindians who came by canoe to buy matches, coca cola, mosquito coils, sardines... Her journey from our house to the stelling, would be by donkey cart, loaded with goods, and we would cadge a ride to the top of the road, legs dangling, filled with the thrill of movement. This my father did not like. Donkey cart? 'Tell your mother she must get Sawh Taxi!' he ordered my mother.

In the posh school with the staircase of haloed Ministers' and Bank Managers' daughters, the questions come hard and fast, *Who are you? Who are you country girl? Country girl with white skin and blue cat-eyes!*

I am boarding with strangers, walking through busy city streets where cars sweep past in morning rain, their windscreen wipers swishing, whose owners think nothing of driving through puddles that fling mud on my bony knees. The teenage daughter of my hosts gathers her friends around her, their laughter cutting me out of the room she is obliged to share with me, my scholarship money poor recompense from a child who hangs her head down, missing home.

That year, my tongue curls up and refuses to speak. It swallows words and hoards them. When people speak to me I cannot answer. Even my fidgety fingers become still.

The joyful exuberance of words pale into the insignificance of me. *Who are you?* I am no one.

Words become intermittent, Morse code to impatient and bemused onlookers. I fail my exams. My father comes to collect me, his face white with shame.

Back home they place a pen into my hand and say, write. On our small town streets, our footprints mark the drying tarmac, kiskadees laugh as we skip with one big rope, all the neighbourhood children, rhyming, jumping, mixing English and Creole, Hindi and Dutch, one word and then two and then three came jumping in. And when my grandmother comes she says, time ah come girl.

And now is the time I know tha't Orealla is a traditional, proud and hardworking Amerindian village on the Corentyne Coast. It's name comes from the Arawak, meaning *white chalk*.

Published Work

LIMBOLANDS (Poetry) Mango Publishing 1999

FROM BERBICE TO BROADSTAIRS (Poetry) Mango Publishing 2006

AFTER A VISIT TO A BOTANICAL GARDENS (Poetry) Cane Arrow Press 2010

KISKADEE GIRL (Memoir) Kingston University Press 2011

CANTERBURY TALES ON A COCKCROW MORNING (Short Fiction) Cultured Llama 2012

IN MARGATE BY LUNCHTIME (Short Fiction) Cultured Llama 2015

SIXTY YEARS OF LOVING (Poetry) Cane Arrow Press 2014

'Sending for Chantal' was the Regional Winner of the Commonwealth Short Story Prize 2014, and was first published by Dundurn Press. Other stories have been published by *The Lampeter Review*, *Poui*, and *WomanSpeak*, ed. Lynn Sweeting.